The Bond Code

THE
B O N D
C O D E

THE DARK
WORLD OF
IAN FLEMING
AND
JAMES BOND

PHILIP GARDINER

NEW PAGE BOOKS
A division of The Career Press, Inc.
Franklin Lakes, NJ

THE BOND CODE
EDITED BY KARA REYNOLDS
TYPESET BY EILEEN DOW MUNSON
Cover design by Dutton and Sherman
Printed in the U.S.A. by Book-mart Press

To order this title, please call toll-free 1-800-CAREER-1 (NJ and Canada: 201-848-0310) to order using VISA or MasterCard, or for further information on books from Career Press.

The Career Press, Inc., 3 Tice Road, PO Box 687,
Franklin Lakes, NJ 07417
www.careerpress.com
www.newpagebooks.com

Library of Congress Cataloging-in-Publication Data
Gardiner, Philip.
    The Bond code : the dark world of Ian Fleming and James Bond / by Philip Gardiner.
        p. cm.
    Includes bibliographical references and index.
    ISBN 978-1-60163-004-9
        1. Fleming, Ian, 1908–1964—Knowledge—Occultism. 2. Fleming, Ian, 1908–1964—
    Characters—James Bond. 3. Bond, James (Fictitious character) 4. Spy stories, English—History and criticism. I. Title.

PR6056.L4Z64 2008
823'.914--dc22

                                                            2007046530

CONTENTS

Introduction

When you make the two one, and when you make the outside like the inside, and the above like the below; when you make the male and female as one, then you will enter the kingdom of God.

—Gospel of Thomas

It was winter and the nights were long, dark, and cold. There was nothing better to do on this particular night than to escape into the world of film with a cup of tea and a biscuit. There was a revival of all things James Bond on the television and in the newspapers, and being a child of the Bond period I sat back and enjoyed a couple of back-to-back films.

I rarely watch television, but sometimes, regardless of what one may think about mind manipulation, commercials, and propaganda, it's nice to relax in front of the TV. At the time I had just finished writing *The Ark, The Shroud, and Mary*, and my mind was once again full of the world of the esoteric, Gnosticism, and the occult. For those who know nothing on the subject, let me explain:

The word *esoteric* means simply knowledge or enlightenment gained by the initiated or educated. It is most often used in relation to secret societies or metaphysical subjects, in which a special or different kind of knowledge is implied—the knowledge of truth, of self, and of balance. The knowledge passed from adept to initiate, from master to pupil, or even (as some would believe) from higher beings to humans, is that of the esoteric. In Greek it is *eis*, meaning "into" or "within," and so the knowledge is that which is gained from within oneself. In this way it is the knowledge, or *gnosis*, spoken of by our ancestors, and is at the heart of all mystery religions.

Again, with the word *occult* we have a knowledge hidden from the profane. Strictly speaking, it is not the knowledge of the supernatural as popularly believed; instead it is simply a knowledge that is hidden, because most cannot see it. Generally this was a knowledge base kept from public view because the Church would use terms such as *heretic* for those who followed the belief that God was within oneself. It was not so long ago that the adept Eliphas Levi (19th century) was imprisoned for stating such things, and so the freedom we have today is a precious and valuable commodity not often known in the history of man. If the masses were to come to the understanding that all they really needed to do in their spiritual life was discover their own self, the intuitive connection to nature, and therefore the Divine within each one of us, then the tithes and will offerings would cease, and the power of the Church would crumble. As it was, and still is to a large extent, the Roman Empire was reborn within the Catholic Church, and so the religion was more about maintaining and growing a power base, rather than liberating the mind and soul of man—it was more about controlling and trapping.

Eliphas Levi

There is a great deal more in my other books about these ancient thought processes, and I do not wish to repeat myself unnecessarily, but now the golden seed of thought has been planted in our minds at the outset of this book, as it needed to be. For what we are about to embark upon is a tale of profound modern occult thought. It is occult, because everybody has missed it, and yet the words and images were placed before us—seen and yet unseen.

These tales of esoteric knowledge were, in the past, placed firmly into fiction, such as those surrounding the search for the Holy Grail, or Robin Hood. Fiction was a wonderful device for hiding truth from those who would kill heretics, and it remains so today. There are a great many statements made in modern fiction. *The (Wonderful) Wizard of Oz* (the book, and, to a large extent, the film) was a statement about the power politics of the world, and was released in the same period that Eliphas Levi was being imprisoned. It may also be said that the silver slippers (changed to ruby in the film) and the yellow/golden brick road journey could be allegories for the alchemical journey.

It was into the world of this early 20th century that Ian Fleming, the creator of James Bond and the child's book *Chitty Chitty Bang Bang*, was born. And this leads me back to that dark winter's night coiled up on the sofa with a cup of tea and my wife. I was watching *Live and Let Die*, with Roger Moore as the famous spy and Jane Seymour as the beautiful Bond girl.

The story struck me as very occult indeed, and started a chain reaction inside my mind—creating a kind of cascade that I simply could not avoid. The story in the film goes that Bond is sent to discover the reason for the murders of three secret service agents in the south of America. While doing so he uncovers a dastardly plot to flood the United States with heroin, and thus create millions of ready-made addicts all needing their daily fix, thus inflating the price. The evildoer is a man by the name of Kananga,[1] a Voodoo-practicing gangster who just happens to be the prime minister of St. Monique in disguise. His weakness becomes Bond's strength, and her name is Solitaire—a Tarot-reading adept who can read a man's soul and predict the future. She and Bond join forces to bring the dualistic madman down and save the world. It struck me that, apart from the myriad occult references in this film (from the book), there was an underlying modern-day fairy tale being played out: Bond was the archetypal hero, the knight in shining armor, riding in and saving the damsel in distress.

The plot is a rehashing of all the other Bond novels, and follows a standard and age-old pattern. As the novelist Umberto Eco explained in *The Rough Guide to James Bond*, the plot goes something like this:

M, the man in charge of MI6, gives a task to James Bond. The villain then makes a move and appears to Bond, who then makes his move, and so on. Following this the woman (Bond girl) makes her move, and is revealed to Bond, who then takes or possesses the girl. Next, the villain captures Bond and tortures him. Our hero then escapes, beats the villain, and unites with the Bond girl.[2]

This underlying plot exists in various forms in all the Bond novels and films, and is the standard upon which Ian Fleming set his character. It is, in effect, the story of a journey, and approaches the magnum opus or "great work" of the alchemist—the work upon the self.

Alchemy

To many, alchemy is a work to transform or transmute a base substance, such as lead, into gold. To others, it is the work to discover the elixir of life. To yet more, it is the work of self-dia*gnosis*—the road we must travel in order to be reborn, resurrected, or renewed. All of these explanations are true, for the alchemists of the past did indeed try to create both the physical and metaphysical ultimate prize. But whether we take the symbolism of the great work literally or metaphorically, the route seems to be the same: It starts with the discovery that the Master (M) reveals to the adept (Bond). The Master passes on certain levels of information for the adept or initiate to work on, and in so doing the adept will find his own path to the truth. On the metaphysical side, in searching for the truth the adept follows the clue laid before him by the Master, and this reveals the darker side of his self—the villain. This is the revelation of Mani, as we shall learn—the dual nature of the self. In order to proceed, the adept must reduce—removing the negative aspects of personality that prevents one from seeing the true self—and be remade, or unite his male and female, positive and negative aspects—the alchemical conjunction. The logical and the emotional must be in unison for the great work of salvation to come to fruition. The reduction (usually torture) may happen more than once, and is in fact a repetitive process of forming and reducing. James Bond, as the alter ego of Ian Fleming, is playing out the role of the alchemist on the screen before us. The reason we do not see this is because it is set in the modern world and not the 16th century.

As I had spent many years reading texts on alchemy, and as I had already written extensively on the work upon the self, it was no surprise that I saw these elements within the Bond character and plots. Nevertheless, when I decided to embark upon the research behind Ian Fleming himself, I was not prepared for what I was to discover.

The stories of James Bond are not just popular spy thrillers. This book you hold is the remarkable tale of how Ian Fleming and his associations with the world of the *occult* actually led him to create a masterful series of clever *clues*, *ciphers*, and *codes* within his novels, revealing a sacred truth he discovered while searching for his own inner harmony.

Some words and concepts may sound strange to the reader, such as *alchemy* and *gnosis*, but in this book I will reveal their truths in a simple step-by-step approach. In fact, the codes within this book will make people radically reappraise other books, such as *The Da Vinci Code.*

We will outline the untold story of Ian Fleming and just why he wrote the James Bond stories. This story must begin with the influences upon the man.

The Influences

▶ During his youth, Ian Fleming was sent to "special" schools in Austria in order to overcome personal issues—issues created by a domineering mother, a dead father, and a successful elder brother. But Fleming fooled everyone, including the doctors.

▶ Ian Fleming explicitly said that Bond was Manichean—a concept perfectly in line with the supposed secrets of certain societies to which Fleming was associated. These are the very same secrets held sacred by secret societies throughout time.

▶ Relatively unknown to the wider world, Ian Fleming actually translated a lecture given by psychoanalyst Carl Jung on the alchemist, physician, and magician, Paracelsus, and we shall run through this text for the first time.

▶ James Bond, as the dragon-slayer of these modern myths, must unite with the feminine principle in order to save the world. This is the secret of the art of alchemy at play, and, along with yet more patterns within the novels, reveals Fleming's understanding of alchemical concepts, as the process of self-improvement and self-knowledge, steeped in hidden language and codes.

▶ Ian Fleming associated with or was influenced by mystics and spiritually inclined individuals, which reveals his inner and hidden thoughts—people such as Rosamond Lehmann, Dame Edith Sitwell (with whom Fleming intended to write a book on the mystic Paracelsus), Aleister Crowley, Sybil Leek, Sefton Delmer, Dennis Wheatley, Sax Rohmer, Dr. John Dee, and Carl Jung. In fact, it is well known that Fleming kept his "groups" quite separate from each other, for secrecy, and with the unraveling of the Bond Code, we will reveal how deep this web of the occult truly went.

Dame Edith Sitwell

The Bond Code

▶ The code 007 (a sacred numerological code) was that of the magician and occultist Dr. John Dee from the 16th century—the infamous mystic and spy of the realm for Queen Elizabeth I.[3]

▶ The queen herself signed her letters to Dee as "M."

▶ Dee was thrown out of university for creating a flying machine—and Fleming wrote the alchemical *Chitty Chitty Bang Bang*. We also know that he was reading a biography of Dee at the time of writing *Casino Royale*, the first Bond novel!

▶ The other number given to Bond, 7777, also has a numerological meaning. Other numerological codes exist here, such as Magic 44.

▶ Fleming named his own retreat Goldeneye, after certain occult terms. The location was known as Oracabessa—the golden head—and is a symbol well-known in alchemical and mystical circles to be the perfected man. Naming the site Goldeneye was also symbolic of the all-seeing eye.

The etymology of the names and words used by Fleming is key. In alchemy, the serpent is a symbol of regeneration and wisdom, but also of negative energy. It is the symbol of dualism, which confronted Fleming throughout his life. The symbolic names include the Ouroboros Fish and Bait Company (an ouroboros is a serpent eating its own tail); Hugo Drax (Drax is dragon, the winged serpent, and Hugo is mind, spirit, or heart); Auric Goldfinger (*auric* is an alchemical term for gold, and the golden finger indicates the alchemist himself, whose finger turns gold through the great work—which is actually known as cheating, something Goldfinger is caught out on a lot); Mr. Big, who was known as "Gallia" (an alchemical metallic substance) and "Kananga" (a Voodoo and Angolan term for water used to purify); Blofeld's network of spies in Tartar (the Greek reference to Hell); Scaramanga (a "caricature of what is within"); and finally, Le Chiffre, *Casino Royale*'s villain, whose name, in Hindi and Sanskrit—the languages of the Eastern philosophers Fleming had read about extensively—is Shunya. This word, *Shunya* or *Sunya*, is a term for the Void or Nothingness. This is not the same nothingness perceived by Western eyes, but a distinct metaphysical reality from where everything comes. It is the source of the true self, and here Fleming is pointing out that the code with Bond is the source of everything. In fact, if one looks deeper into the word, one finds that it means the absolute, attainment, realization, and enlightenment, and is often imaged with the "third eye."

▶ Bond himself is related to the serpent. His wife, Tracey, was known as Draco (the dragon or winged serpent).

In short, Fleming lived in a fantasy world in order to escape his own inner turmoil—something that led him to his death through smoking 70 cigarettes a day and drinking copious amounts of alcohol. This fantasy world led him into the land of the occult and gnostic thought. He created his fantasy alter-ego as a great alchemical work to occupy his own chaotic mind, just as many before have done. But he left behind a set of clues and codes for us to decipher—just as our medieval friends did hundreds of years ago.

We shall also discover that Fleming associated with radical secret societies, both while within the secret service and in post-war Britain.

The very codes left by Ian Fleming within his work are the codes to the secrets of these societies.

Some of the occult links within the pages of this book are proven or provable, and others are conjecture, based upon the many influences on and references in Fleming and his work. The problem is that Ian Fleming kept his friends quite apart from each other—keeping his secrets well-guarded. Another thing Fleming did was to give several reasons for his characters' names and actions, often changing his mind or finding some new place to which he could divert attention. This is well documented by all biographers, but nobody has asked the question, why? What purpose did Fleming have in this diversion? What was he hiding? Because some of these conjectures may seem a little far-fetched on occasion, I have marked the "long-shots" with an asterisk (*) to show where new evidence is needed to be fully proven. I included these theories for the reader to consider because new evidence may come to light in the future.

CHAPTER 1

IAN FLEMING, PART I: A BRIEF BIOGRAPHY

Ian Lancaster Fleming was born in Mayfair, London, to Valentine Fleming and Evelyn St. Croix-Rose Fleming on May 28, 1908. He died on August 12, 1964. His father was once a member of the British Parliament (he died in action in the Great War), and his mother descended from royal blood. His elder brother, Peter Fleming, would go on to become one of the world's most famous travel writers, and, before Bond became popular, Peter unintentionally eclipsed everything Ian did.

Ian Fleming was born into the class of Englishmen for whom every option is open, and yet he managed to single-handedly close them down. The Fleming family was wealthy, not least because his grandfather, Robert Fleming, was a successful Scottish banker—the family company being sold for $7 billion. However, Valentine Fleming's will and testament stipulated that Evelyn would only retain the family wealth so long as she never remarried, and this caused ongoing family issues throughout Ian's life. Another issue was the ghost of his father as the erudite parliamentarian and war hero. Ian Fleming grew from the age of 8 without his father and under the dominance of his overbearing mother. The children used to say prayers and ask God that they be as good as their father. Unfortunately, Ian Fleming could not live up to these ideals, and failed to be both a parliamentarian, which he did once run for, and an action war hero. On the other hand, his brother, Peter, succeeded, and indeed excelled in everything he did, from sports to writing and even the role of all-action war hero.

Ian Fleming, always with a cigarette

Ian Fleming's education at Eton didn't go as well as his elders brother's extraordinary success, so he was moved to a "more convenient" situation at the Royal Military Academy at Sandhurst, although he had won Victor Ludorum (Latin for "Winner of Games") at Eton two years running. To the annoyance of his mother, he didn't much take to Sandhurst, so she sent him abroad to "learn languages." He went to Austria, where he spent time at Kitzbuhel with the Adlerian disciple Forbes Dennis and his American wife, Phyllis Bottome. The cover story was that he went to improve his German and other languages, but it was really an attempt to fix this troublesome teenager. Following his time in Austria, he moved on and eventually disappointed everybody by finding a job as a sub-editor and journalist at the Reuters news agency. Later on he also worked as a stockbroker with Rowe and Pitman in Bishopsgate. At this time he took up residence in Belgravia, at 22B Ebury Street, to be exact, where he spent his time entertaining friends at dinner parties. He attempted to live the high life without the financial means, and he always seemed to offer up a façade that fooled everybody. Inside himself, he was bored. The stock market offered no great excitement, and he obviously envied his globe-trotting journalistic brother. He collected books and started to grow an extensive network of friends that would prove useful for his future life as a novelist, not least because they gave him a list of characters from which to choose.

Friends in the foreign office arranged for an exciting excursion for the young Fleming in 1939, and sent him off to Russia under the auspices of reporting for the *Times* newspaper. In fact, he was spying for the foreign office the whole time, and other journalists spotted the ruse but remained quiet.

By May 1939, war had broken out across Europe, and Britain was preparing for some of the bloodiest battles in its history. Ian Fleming needed a role, and was soon recruited by Rear Admiral John Godfrey, director of Naval intelligence, to be his personal assistant. Fleming moved from Royal Naval volunteer reserve lieutenant to lieutenant commander and then finally to commander—the rank he would eventually give to James Bond. It seemed that the peculiar, arrogant, imaginative, and forthright nature that was Ian Fleming, worked well for military intelligence just so long as it was kept on a leash. He worked tirelessly throughout the war, and got to know every section well. Being personal assistant to the rear admiral was a huge responsibility, and Fleming took to the role well, making sure he knew everything he possibly could, soaking it up like a sponge and storing it all unwittingly for later Bond novels. It was even at this time that Fleming managed to develop his literary skill by producing daily situation reports and regular memos—many of which read like Bond novels. He eventually contributed work to the Political Warfare Executive, the Joint Intelligence Committee, the Special Operations Executive, and the Secret Intelligence Service.

Between 1941 and 1942, Rear Admiral Godfrey, along with Fleming, made secret trips to the United States in order to open and maintain dialog between the various and newly formed intelligence agencies there, meeting such classic figures as J. Edgar Hoover and William Stephenson. In 1941, the American general William Donovan asked Fleming to write a memorandum outlining the structure of a proposed secret service. This set Fleming's mind racing, and his imagination into overdrive. He completed the task, and was awarded a .38 Police Positive Colt pistol for his services, inscribed "For Special Services." The memorandum Fleming penned was actually used in part when the OSS was organized. The OSS, or Office of Strategic Services, was the U.S. intelligence agency formed during the Second World War, and would later help to create the CIA.

Ian Fleming

Fleming also traveled to Ceylon, Jamaica, Australia, France, Spain, and North Africa, visiting embassies and setting up Operation Goldeneye, which he named, to defend Gibralter.

By 1942, Ian Fleming had secured authority to set up his own elite spy-commando unit known as 30 AU (30 Auxiliary Unit), which he nick-named "Red Indians." The men were trained very much like the later

James Bond, with lock-picking, explosives, firearms, and combat train-ing. They were all-round intelligent and brave men, and were in fact the real and original James Bond characters, being sent in to enemy terri-tory in order to extricate ciphers and weapons of interest. They were so successful that Fleming managed to grow them in sufficient size and strength that by the end of the war they were almost too powerful a group to be led by a mere commander, and Fleming began to lose con-trol of them to higher-ranking officers.

After the war, Fleming didn't immediately begin to write books. In-stead he went back into journalism and ended up at the *Times*. He spent his time socializing with various groups that he kept quite separate, and some secret; continued collecting books, including first editions of *Mein Kampf* and *On the Origin of Species*; and finding a new part-time home in Jamaica, which he renamed Goldeneye. By 1953, he plucked up the cour-age to finally write his first novel, and published *Casino Royale*. The book had a slow start, causing Fleming to wonder if the books would ever take off. So he did what all good authors have to do: He hustled. It eventually paid off, and the U.S. market opened up for him, and sales soared.

He now began a routine that was to continue for the rest of his short life: In January each year he flew to Jamaica to avoid the bitter English weather and write his novels. He remained there until March, when he would return and take up his normal day job at the Kemsley newspaper empire. Then he met Lady Anne Rothermere, and they fell in love, and were indeed lovers for several years. Anne eventually became pregnant with Fleming's child, so she divorced Lord Rothermere and married Ian Fleming. She gave birth to Caspar, Ian's only son, who himself died in 1975.

Fleming's circle of friends was incredible, and no one has ever written them all down, for he kept them all quite separate from one another. The list includes such great names as Noel Coward, Cyril Connolly, Edith Sitwell, William Plomer, Peter Quennell, Raymond Chandler, Kingsley Amis, and even the American "royals," the Kennedys. At one time, his home in Jamaica was used by the prime minister of Great Britain, Anthony Eden, to recover from an illness.

Noel Coward

Fleming wrote 12 novels and nine short stories in total, all featuring the infamous suave and sophisticated super spy. Many people are surprised to discover that Fleming also wrote the children's novel *Chitty Chitty Bang Bang*, because the film was adapted by Roald Dahl, and is quite different from the book.

By 1961, Fleming had sold the film rights for all his Bond books, present and future, to Harry Saltzman. With Albert R. "Cubby" Broccoli, Saltzman made the first Bond film, *Dr. No*, in 1962, with Sean Connery in the lead. Fleming had actually wanted David Niven, his close friend, and had also asked that his second-cousin Christopher Lee be considered for the part of Dr. No:

> He said to me, "One of my books is to be filmed. Have you ever read Dr. No?" I said that was good news and,

yes, I had. "I want you to play Dr. No, if you will. You'd suit the part," he said. Well, Dr. No at 6-foot-6 tops me by a couple of inches, but then he wore lifts. Dr. No had steel hands, possibly inspired by the hands I wore in Hands of Orlac, and he was a sinister Oriental, as I had been often enough. So it all seemed quite logical, not merely the idle fancy of a cousin, to pick me for Dr. No. "Great," I said, "wonderful!" "I've asked them to offer you the part," he said.[1]

Sir Sean Connery as James Bond

Of course, everyone who has seen the films will know that Christopher Lee did not in fact get the part of Dr. No, but sometime after the death of Ian Fleming he was asked to play Scaramanga in *The Man With the Golden Gun*.

Ian Fleming only lived long enough to see the second Bond film, *From Russia With Love*, released in 1963. For decades he had smoked more than 60 cigarettes a day, and drank all manner of alcohol. His doctor once insisted that he reduce his daily alcohol intake and cut the cigarettes by 10, from 70. But as Fleming put it, "I would rather that my spark should burn out in a brilliant blaze than it should be stifled by dry rot. I would rather be a superb meteor, every atom of me in a magnificent glow, than a sleeping and permanent planet. The proper function of life is to live, not to exist. I shall not waste my days in trying to prolong them. I shall use the time."[2]

Ian Fleming's impression of James Bond

In 1964 he suffered a severe chest cold combined with pleurisy, and this forced him to consider a slow recovery. This was beyond his mind, in the same way that a speedy recovery was beyond his body. Instead he slowed down a little, but still went to meetings at the *Times* where he worked. In fact he was said to have forced himself to attend the Royal St. George's golf club at Sandwich committee meeting, and even stayed on for lunch afterwards. However, that same night he claimed to be in "great despair," and by the following day his hemorrhage was so bad that he was rushed to Canterbury Hospital.

Ian Fleming died on August 12, 1964, of a heart attack in Canterbury Hospital, Kent, at the all-too-young age of 56. He was buried in the church-yard cemetery of Sevenhampton near Swindon, England. In 1975, his son, Caspar, joined his father, and in 1981 his widow, Anne, did the same.

CHAPTER 2

THE BOND NOVELS

James Bond, with two double bourbons inside him, sat in the final departure lounge of Miami Airport and thought about life and death.

—Ian Fleming,
opening line from *Goldfinger*

Now that we know a little about Ian Fleming, and we understand a little about the role of fairy tales and the esoteric world, it's time to take a brief walk through the Bond novels and short stories to garner an overall feeling of the theme—one of stark and yet hidden realities from within the mind of a divided and yet intelligent man.

As we have already discovered, there is a constant thread, or pattern, running through the Bond stories, of awakening or interest piqued, confrontation with the darkest fear, union and resolution. Understanding and being aware of these patterns will open up a new world before us as we unravel the Bond Code. In the following paragraphs I will include some hints regarding various characters, with the etymological meaning of the name given in parentheses.

Most people will be aware of James Bond purely from the films. They will have grown up with Roger Moore, George Lazenby, Sean Connery, Pierce Brosnan, and, of course, Daniel Craig, who began his Bond career with *Casino Royale*—the very first Bond novel.

Casino Royale

Released on April 13, 1953, in the United Kingdom, and in 1955 in the United States, this was the first Bond novel written by Ian Fleming and the second Bond film directed by Martin Campbell, who also directed Pierce Brosnan's first Bond film, *Goldeneye*. Fleming's first titles for the book were *The Double-O Agent* and *The Deadly Gamble*, but were disregarded in favor of *You Asked for It* and subtitled *Casino Royale*. By 1960 the subtitle had replaced *You Asked for It*.

The plot has the Soviet assassination bureau SMERSH raising funds at the baccarat table at a French casino, with the villain Le Chiffre doing all the playing. Bond as the double-o agent and expert baccarat player is sent in to put a stop to the fundraising efforts by beating Le Chiffre. With the aid of U.S. money and CIA agent Felix Leiter, Bond manages to ruin Le Chiffre (the cipher, or code). However, he also has a female assistant by the name of Vesper Lynd (birth of night), who also just happens to be a Russian agent who betrays her loyalty to the Soviet Union in order to help Bond. However, Bond is captured by Le Chiffre and tortured, only to be saved by SMERSH agents who are called in to kill Le Chiffre. They set Bond free after marking him with an S for "spy" on his left hand. The S, we are told, is Cyrillic, from the language of St. Cyril, a devoted Christian who gave himself up to the pursuit of heavenly wisdom at the age of 7.

Bond then spends three weeks in convalescence with Vesper Lynd, where he expresses his wish to leave the service. However, Lynd's past catches up with her as SMERSH agent Gettler (Germanic for *God* from *got*) is seen prowling, and Lynd commits suicide. Bond, having overcome so much in his union with this feminine principle, then has to suffer the consequences of what is sown, and must begin the process again.

It seems nobody can escape their past, for God will catch up with you. All we can do is purge the soul. This is at the heart of the Bond Code.

According to Fleming's famous understatements and off-the-cuff explanations, he wrote *Casino Royale* to take his mind off his forthcoming marriage to Lady Rothermere. Fleming was well-known for explaining things away with simple statements, and often contradicted himself. It may be that the book was written during the period before his marriage, and that the success of this union was playing upon his mind, but the fact remains that his (and others') statements reveal that he had been piecing together the elements of *Casino Royale* in his mind for some time. In the book, Fleming reveals that he needs the feminine principle to see the job through, but struggles with the negative side of this concept. He is showing how he himself struggled with the concept of having to offer up himself as a virtual sacrifice to the union, both physically to his future wife, and internally to the emotional element within himself, and not just the clean, crisp, logical mind he wished to portray to the wider world. This is very much an element also found within the life of the occultist and associate of Fleming, Aleister Crowley, misunderstood on the whole by many commentators as a disliking of females.

Aleister Crowley

The introduction of Le Chiffre is also the first glimpse we have of Fleming's interest in the infamous Aleister Crowley. The novel's physical description of Le Chiffre matches that of Crowley, and it is believed by Bond lovers the world over that the villains in Fleming's novels were all based upon this "devilish" character.

Live and Let Die

Released in 1954, *Live and Let Die* sees Bond given instructions to go to New York City and investigate the gangster Mr. Big, who operates from Harlem and Florida. It is believed that Mr. Big is selling gold coins discovered in Jamaica from the horde of the infamous pirate Sir Henry Morgan. Our villain is again an agent of SMERSH, and is using the revenue to fund Soviet spy operations. Bond meets up with his happy helper, Felix Leiter, and they are both captured and tortured by Mr. Big. Bond unites with Mr. Big's fortune-telling weakness, Solitaire, and they escape to Florida. Solitaire is captured, Leiter is fed to the sharks and loses a leg and an arm, and Bond travels to Jamaica, where he joins up with Querrel and John Strangways. In the end, Bond places a limpet mine on Mr. Big's boat, but is captured, tied up with Solitaire, and dragged across a coral reef before the limpet mine finally explodes and saves the day.

A pattern is again obvious in this tale, which is a common theme of alchemy: the task, the reduction, and the reformation. But also implicit in this tale is the Voodoo theme, something Ian Fleming became very interested in, as it revealed the same ancient processes spoken of in alchemy.

The use of gold coins as the catalyst, or reason for the endeavour in the story, speaks of Fleming's possible relation to Crowley directly, the true "grand master of esoteric magick" himself. I am privy to Crowley lore via author O.H. Krill, a Crowley expert, who said:

Regardless of any preconceived notion of this man, he has influenced countless great minds of the last 100 years and is responsible for our ability to travel into space among many other things. It would appear that Fleming knew of Crowley's ways at least to a degree, as he was never without very, very old gold coins whenever possible. More on this I cannot say, but I believe that Fleming has weaved his most powerful influences into his books, I dare say these influences might be somewhat responsible for the magic and sustainability to his works.

Aleister Crowley

Originally called *The Undertaker's Wind*, *Live and Let Die* was Ian Fleming's attempt to write a more serious book. In later life he suggested, in his usual off-hand fashion and self-deprecating way (such self-ridicule distanced himself from the critics whom he knew misunderstood his intent), that his books were mere entertainment, but he did begin with serious intentions. Many biographers and critics have stated that Fleming was actually "meditating, through Mr. Big, on the nature of evil."[1] What we shall learn as we progress is that Ian Fleming was playing out the turmoil of his own mind within the reworkings of the age-old fairytale genre. His own grasping after the ancient psychological methods of self-improvement, known to many as gnosis, was laid bare before us—at least if we have the eyes to see. Most people, however, come to these tales looking for a spy novel, and of course that is exactly what they get. Those perceptions cloud the view. The tales of the Holy Grail are all too often claimed to be some kind of real search for a real object (or even the bloodline of Jesus), and this too clouds the true meaning behind the story— that of the great work of the alchemists, or the true connection to the Divine of the Gnostics, Sufis, and numerous others.

Fleming gained much of his insight for *Live and Let Die* from a book called *The Traveller's Tree* by Patrick Leigh Fermor, whom he names in the novel, and whom he knew from his intelligence days, as Fermor had been an intelligence officer in the Irish Guards. Fermor was an erudite travel writer of the first order, and had a deep knowledge and interest in the myths, mysteries, and occult world of the places he visited. This enthusiasm comes through in his wonderful books, and for Fleming it was a breath of fresh air that gave him impetus to write *Live and Let Die* in the style in which he did. In *Mani*, Fermor revels in the subtle psychology of the mythologies of Greece, and, similar to Fleming, hides a lot of what he is really saying behind metaphor. There is an excellent chapter on the little village of Areopolis, the gateway to the Inner Mani, that reveals this concept beautifully. The cover itself is adorned with the solar golden third eye.

Sufi mystic

In Fermor's book *The Traveller's Tree*, he points out the similarities between the Haitian Voodoo cults and rituals and those of ancient Egypt, and Fleming copied this understanding into his own novel, quoting Fermor word for word as Bond reads the book, stating: "Haitian ethnologists connect with the rejuvenation rites of Osiris recorded in the Book of the Dead."

Indeed, in a method markedly similar to that of Osiris and Horus, or even the Shamanic beliefs, Bond undergoes a tortuous scene in which his arms are fastened to a chair, and Tee-Hee (Mr. Big's henchman) is ordered to take off his little finger, bending it back so far that it eventually snaps. It is a part of Shamanic lore that in order to access the other world and gain insight, the Shaman must lose some part of the body, or be broken and scarred. This is giving up something as payment, and Bond does so in almost every book.

In this book, Fleming is playing with the world of the paranormal, as if philosophically joining the debate with the use of Solitaire and Bond. Bond says that Solitaire thinks he would not understand the Voodoo ways, but he explains that he knows the root of fear and what it can do. He claims to have read most of the books on Voodoo, and believes that it works through the fear within the mind. But Solitaire counters him, wanting him to at least believe that Mr. Big is in reality the zombie of Baron Samedi himself—the Prince of Darkness and Death, who has psychic powers. Bond promises Solitaire that he will cut a cross in his bullet and shoot Mr. Big to ensure his death, and they agree—the union of the male and female has resolved the issue of the dark side. This is followed by the alchemical *conjunctio*—the physical and mental union of the male and female as Bond and Solitaire make love. In the alchemical terminology, Solitaire is the watery, wise Sophia of the Gnostics, and Bond is the fire. The picture is painted with Solitaire's hair falling in a "cascade," and Bond being described as an "angry flame."

Incredibly, later in the book Fleming goes off on a philosophical tour of consciousness, examining man's connection to all nature and all things. He explains how Bond's thoughts wander into this world while overcoming the fear of flying: "The whole of life is cutting through the pack with death," he explains, and "[y]our stars have already let you come quite a long way since you left your mothers womb."

Any happy landing simply comes to Bond by courtesy of the stars, revealing a distinct belief in astrology, which, as we shall find, had a strong influence upon Ian Fleming. Bond's stated ultimate prize was not overcoming Mr. Big, nor finding the treasure, but Solitaire, who had helped him to break the code! And yet, he could still not work out the greatest of puzzles—the secret of the stars: "The stars winked down their cryptic morse and he had no key to their cipher."

Moonraker

Published in 1955, *Moonraker* was the third novel by Ian Fleming, and has little resemblance to the film of the same name starring Roger Moore. In fact, it more closely resembles *Die Another Day* with Pierce Brosnan. The title is a synonym for the *moonsail*, the highest sail on a ship, and the moon by which we navigate. It also refers to the folk tale from Wiltshire, England, about how the locals hid contraband from the officials in a pond, and, when asked why they were raking the water, claimed that they were trying to catch the light of the moon.

Again the story begins with M giving Bond his instructions. He is to observe and report on the activities of Sir Hugo Drax (mind of the dragon/serpent), who appears to be winning too much money playing bridge at Blades, which just happens to be M's gentleman's club. M suspects Drax of cheating, and is perplexed that a millionaire would stoop so low. Bond takes on the challenge, and actually defeats Drax at his own cheating game, and thus the battle ensues.

It turns out that Drax is actually plotting to destroy London using his Moonraker missile project, and so Bond has to save the day by uniting with the feminine principle Gala Brand (merry fire). The enemy within is there yet again with Hugo Drax (Bond's arch-nemesis), and Bond saves the day while in perfect union with his feminine principle—the Bond girl.

Diamonds Are Forever

Published in 1956, this story begins with Bond only two months after *Moonraker* finishes, and while recovering from injuries received during that case. M is tipped off about a diamond-smuggling ring, and gives Bond instructions to infiltrate the gang and find out who is behind it all. He quickly goes undercover and meets his new Bond girl, Tiffany Case (manifestation fallen from God). He then discovers that the mob responsible for the smuggling is known as the Spangled Mob, run by Jack Spang and Seraffimo Spang (shiny). Bond uncovers the intricate smuggling operation, and discovers that it leads all the way to Las Vegas, where he is revealed as a spy by the mob, who then set about torturing him. He escapes with the help of Tiffany and Felix Leiter (happy helper), and the diamond pipeline is destroyed.

In this book we have Fleming's fascination with the diamond-smuggling industry, treasure troves, and piracy. All biographers agree that Fleming introduced these themes into his formula because of his interest and recent journalistic forays into the diamond industry, and yet it is little known that he was also deeply interested in the world of the occult, and so also included occult themes in his works.

Bond's own introduction into the world of diamonds is similar to the journey into the world of the alchemists' Philosopher's Stone: "It was domination by a beauty so pure that it held a kind of truth, a divine authority before which all other material things turned, like the bit of quartz, to clay. In these few minutes Bond understood the myth of diamonds, and he knew that he would never forget what he had suddenly seen inside the heart of this stone."

There is a code here at play, one so beautiful and simple that it is easy to walk by. Bond is given this wonderful insight into pure truth by his boss, M—it is the master passing on a vision to the initiate, to further his work. Bond would never again forget what he had seen while gazing into the depth of the stone, and this statement would be as relevant to any alchemist throughout time, and understood as such. Today, many people have no concept of what alchemy is, let alone the intricacies of it, as understood by Fleming from the very earliest of his influences. To stare into the beauty of the stone in alchemical terms is to look upon the face of the source of creation—to see the light of God, the Divine—and Bond's task was now to go out into the world and track down the darkness that would keep the light from the rest of mankind, and destroy it. We are all to work through the Philosopher's Stone—through the light of the Divine.

It was with this vision that Bond was able to progress into the dark world itself and have "faith in his sixth sense," as Fleming points out in the book. Death, says Bond, is forever, but so too are diamonds.

From Russia With Love

Published in 1957, this is the fifth book in the series, and most critics claim that it is the pinnacle of Fleming's Bond novels—either because John F. Kennedy included it in his list of favorite books, or the complexity of the storyline. The plot is complex, but we shall quickly run over it here: The Soviet organization known as SMERSH decides to set a trap for Bond, and kill him "with ignominy." The plot fails mainly because the trap is laid with a young cipher agent named Tatiana Romanova, who actually does fall for Bond, and they take part in Gypsy rituals and lovemaking. The complex twists and turns, involving Rosa Klebb (bread and wine), a chess master, and various red herrings still hide the same plotline, whereby Bond must unite with the feminine in order to overcome his adversary—although he does suffer a poisoning at the end of this book, and we are left wondering whether he will survive or not. Other characters include the head of the British secret service in Turkey, Darko Kerim Bey (gift of great wonderment), and Red Grant (red creed).

Dr. No

The next novel and first real Bond movie was *Dr. No*, published in 1958, and largely inspired by the Fu Manchu character of Sax Rohmer, whom we shall discover heavily influenced Fleming. In many respects it is also a reprise of *Live and Let Die*. In this novel, Bond is still recovering from the fights in his previous assignment, so M gives him a simple task: investigate the disappearance of the head secret service operative in Jamaica—John Strangways. Foul play is suspected of a local bird-dung merchant who happens to own an island nearby, called Crab Key, where there is believed to be a fire-breathing dragon. Dr. Julius No, the dung-merchant, is Chinese-German, uniting Fu Manchu and Fleming's Nazi knowledge. Bond joins up with Querrel and Honeychile Rider (Bond girl), and discovers that Dr. No is in fact working for the Soviets and is set on sabotaging nearby American missile tests. Bond and Bond girl are caught and tortured, with Dr. No saying, "You have both put me

to a great deal of trouble. Now I intend to put you to a great deal of pain."
Poor old Querrel is burned to death by the dragon (a mechanical creation
of Dr. No).

Bond is taken to Dr. No's underworld and underwater lair. Bond
equates him with the serpent, and so he must slay the dragon to escape.
This is a metaphor for the unconscious realm, where the true soul must
do battle to overcome the dangers of the shadow self and be free again
to see the light. In the end, Bond overcomes Dr. No, and, with Honeychile,
he kills him and saves the day. But he could only do this in union with the
feminine principle—the wisdom of Sophia: "He thought of the girl and
the thought gave him strength. He wasn't dead yet. Damn it, he wouldn't
die! Not until the heart was torn from his body."

He can only do this, save himself and win the day, by submerging
himself in wisdom and washing himself clean of all sin—the alchemical
journey toward resurrection, and, phoenix-like, Bond must rise again.
"Hang on to life.... To hell with what happened just now. Get down into
the water and wash!"

Goldfinger

Bond is called on to investigate cheating in a game of Canasta by
our villain Auric Goldfinger (an alchemical name—see Chapter 10), in
Miami. Goldfinger is caught cheating by Bond and forced to pay back his
winnings. Upon returning to London, Bond researches Goldfinger and
finds out that he is a gold smuggler, and the treasurer of SMERSH. Bond
is sent to collect information and contact Goldfinger in a high-takes game
of golf, in which Goldfinger again cheats, but is duped by Bond and loses.
Bond's new mission now is to try and recover the smuggled gold, and

while doing so he uncovers a plot to steal gold bullion from Fort Knox. With the help of Felix Leiter and Pussy Galore (Bond girl) he foils Goldfinger's scheme and saves the day.

For Your Eyes Only

This is not a novel, but a collection of short stories including "From a View to a Kill," "For Your Eyes Only," "Quantum of Solace" (originally in *Cosmopolitan*), "Risico," and "The Hildebrand Rarity" (originally in *Playboy*). Instead of being the normal run-of-the-mill spy thrillers, these are tales mostly of ordinary people and ordinary lives interspersed with intrigue and darkness. In "The Hildebrand Rarity" Bond watches as a wife kills her brutal husband; in "Quantum of Solace" he listens to tales of ordinary people and real-life drama. "For Your Eyes Only" follows the standard plot of M sending Bond on a mission, but this time the Bond girl kills the main villain before Bond has a chance. "From a View to a Kill" has Bond trapping an assassin. These are, in effect, collected thoughts of Ian Fleming played out in five very different stories.

Thunderball

The start of this novel reveals some of the Fleming in Bond, as M informs him that his overindulgence in cigarettes and drink is ruining his health. And so Bond is sent on a two-week vacation to Shrublands health farm in the countryside. There, he comes across a certain Count Lippe (Germanic for *lip*—the edge of something), who seems to have a link with the Red Lightning Tong—a secret criminal organization from Macao, China. Lippe discovers that Bond has deduced his connections, and so tries to kill him, but fails.

When Bond returns to London, having been through the trial of death, he is said to be a "new man," as if reborn. Almost immediately the secret service receives a message from SPECTRE (Special Executive for Counter-intelligence, Terrorism, and Extortion) claiming to have hijacked a V Bomber with two nuclear bombs on board. They demand £100,000,000, or they will destroy a major city. The SPECTRE number-one and creator is Ernst Stavro Blofeld (earnest strong), who was, more than incidentally, born on the same day as Ian Fleming, thus revealing Fleming's feelings—that he was fighting out his own issues on paper. As if to further endorse this, Blofeld's right-hand man is Emilio Largo, which means "slow rival."

A joint U.S. and UK operation is launched, called Operation Thunderball, and Bond is sent by M to the Bahamas to investigate a hunch. Bond joins up with Felix Leiter and meets Largo's mistress, Dominetta Vitali (flying mask), whom he turns into his own spy. Dominetta is captured by Largo and tortured. Bond and Leiter chase Largo's boat with a submarine, ending with a short battle and Bond almost being killed by Largo, but Dominetta saves him by firing a spear into Largo's neck. Bond and Dominetta are united and save the day.

The Spy Who Loved Me

This is the 10th and shortest Bond novel, released in 1962, and is very sexually explicit. It is in fact a peculiar departure from the ordinary Bond novel. It is told in the first person by Vivienne Michel (great water goddess), who is rescued from two savage mobsters who are attempting to burn down her house. Fleming was reputedly unhappy with the novel, and only gave permission for the title to be used as a film, and not the content.

Fleming wrote this prologue to the book, which some critics claim was his attempt to distance himself from it:

> I found what follows lying on my desk one morning. As you will see, it appears to be the first-person story of a young woman, evidently beautiful and not unskilled in the arts of love. According to her story, she appears to have been involved, both perilously and romantically, with the same James Bond whose secret-service exploits I myself have written from time to time. With the manuscript was a note signed "Vivienne Michel" assuring me that what she had written was "purest truth and from the depths of her heart.

The truth may be that Fleming was embarrassed by very feminine tale interspersed with thriller interludes, but is there more to the story? It may be, similar to many esoteric writers before him, that the words of "Sophia" are attributed to the goddess herself, who in this instance is named etymologically the "great water/wisdom goddess." *Michel* is *Michael* and means "great," and Vivienne is the water goddess of wisdom (water in the feminine form is linked with wisdom—the watery depths of the mind). Choosing the name for the heroine must always be one of the writer's hardest things to do, and here Fleming has chosen one of the great water goddess, Co-Vianna, or Coventina. This water goddess was the origination of the Lady of the Lake from Arthurian legend, otherwise known as Nimue or the white serpent. Water deities are linked inextricably to the ancient worship of the serpent, because of the wisdom element—the water was a symbol of the unconscious realm, as the psychoanalyst, Carl Jung, who inspired Fleming, pointed out.

There is little doubt that Fleming knew the meaning behind the name he penned, and I believe that Fleming is releasing here, in his later years, the feminine principle he struggled with during his logical life. This water goddess was releasing wisdom from the "purest truth and from the depths of her heart."

On Her Majesty's Secret Service

Published in 1963, this was the 11th book in the series and the second in the Blofeld trilogy. Bond is so frustrated after spending a year looking for Ernst Stavro Blofeld that he actually sends a letter of resignation to M. In the meantime, he meets a suicidal young woman by the name of Teresa de Vicenzo, the daughter of Marc-Ange Draco, the head of Europe's biggest crime syndicate. Marc-Ange Draco offers Bond a huge dowry, and the whereabouts of Blofeld, if he marries Teresa to save her from her mental problems. Bond refuses, but does agree to romance Teresa, and so is given the whereabouts of Blofeld, who now lives in Switzerland under a new name. This is also proof that Fleming played around with the etymology of names, for Blofeld is now Bleuville— from "blue field" or "blue town." Bond infiltrates Blofeld's lair atop Piz Gloria and finds that Blofeld has opened a mental health institute to cure young ladies of allergies and phobias. The whole thing turns out to be a cover for brainwashing the ladies into carrying out a devastating biological attack on Britain's agriculture.

Bond believes his cover is blown, and so escapes, proposes to Teresa, and returns to Piz Gloria with Marc-Ange Draco's men to destroy Piz Gloria. Blofeld escapes, but has his moment of glory when he murders Teresa Bond just after their wedding.

The book certainly has a number of name-codes included: Marc-Ange Draco is broken up into *mars*, *angel*, and *dragon*. Sable Basilisk, a character Bond meets at the College of Arms, is a play on the red/rouge dragon—the title of a junior officer at the real College of Arms, and named after the red dragon of Wales. It is well known that Fleming was deeply interested in the origin of names and played with them extensively. It is also true that Fleming was deeply interested in codes and ciphers. At the time of writing *On Her Majesty's Secret Service*, Fleming was aided by the heraldry expert, Robin de la Lanne-Mirrlees, and it is said they were good friends. This interesting character was a knight of the Sovereign Military Hospitaller Order of St. John of Jerusalem of Rhodes and of Malta, and had various connections that would have intrigued Fleming. Of course, these Knights of Malta are renowned for their own intrigue and connections to the ill-fated Knights Templar.

You Only Live Twice

Bond's career is dwindling fast. He has lost his wife—his feminine principle—and is starting to fall apart. M even considers taking him out of the service altogether, but instead decides to "promote" him to the diplomatic side of the secret service. Bond is even given a new number: 7777. To understand this number we have to delve a little deeper.

The last entry in the New Testament is Revelation 22:21, "The grace of our Lord Jesus Christ be with you all. Amen." Every letter has a number, and this is known as *numerology* or *gematria*. The number of the characters in this case just happens to work out at 7777, with a very peculiar meaning: "It is done." This happens to be the final Bond novel published while Fleming was still alive. However, in this novel Fleming has a very Japanese flavor, and so if we look at Eastern numerology we find that the four 7s are significant. They represent the absolute limit, the end, more than we can know. This knowledge of numbers or gematria is without doubt part of the Bond Code and reveals that Fleming's great work, similar to that of the alchemist, was coming to an end. The influences on Fleming throughout his life show that he could have gained this knowledge from a number of people, not least of whom may have been Aleister Crowley, who had written a book entitled *777 and Other Qabalistic Writings*.

Fleming includes another clue in the book. Bond's new mission is to fly to Japan and persuade Tiger Tanaka (dwelling tiger, which represents the lineage of warriors or Samurai), the head of the Japanese secret service, to divulge information about an informant from within the Soviet Union who goes by the title of Magic 44. In numerology, the number 44 is the balance between the spiritual and physical—the very element Fleming had struggled with his whole life, and in this novel he was searching in code for the secret. It is the mystery of the mental state and the material world—true magic, searched for by Fleming, his alter-ego Bond, and indeed the very first Bond, magician and numerologist Dr. John Dee.

To find the secret of Magic 44, Tanaka asks Bond to assassinate Dr. Guntram (war raven) Shatterhand, who runs the politically embarrassing Garden of Death—a place for people to go and commit suicide in peace—sometimes whether they wish to or not. Incredibly, Bond takes the mission and discovers that Shatterhand is his arch-rival, Blofeld, and so the full circle is complete, and the end in sight. Bond is aided once again by a beautiful Bond girl, this time named Kissy Suzuki, and with the help of makeup and training he manages to be reborn as Japanese, renamed Taro Todoroki (first-born thunder, which is symbolized by the dragon, so Bond is the first-born dragon, as was Arthur and many heroes from folklore).

Bond eventually meets his nemesis, and they duel. Blofeld is killed, but Bond suffers amnesia from a blow to the head, and the world believes him dead. However, he is in fact living life as a Japanese fisherman with Kissy Suzuki. The union between the two results in Kissy becoming pregnant. However, Bond is never told of the pregnancy, and discovers a piece of paper with the word *Vladivostok* on it, and this triggers him to seek out his past. Fleming never resolved the issue of the pregnancy.

At the end of the book, M writes Bond's obituary, which, not surprisingly, is the obituary of Ian Fleming.

This novel is, for me, one of the best, because its twists and turns reveal the mind of Fleming on paper. It is the tale of a rebirthing and resurrection, with a distinct sense of having finally arrived, only to then lose everything again. I get the sense that Fleming felt very much the same way—that he never quite managed to attain his goals.

The Man With the Golden Gun

In the last novel (the book of short stories, *Octopussy and the Living Daylights*, was published after Fleming's death) we are left wondering what has happened to Bond. He was presumed dead, but then a man appears in London claiming to be Bond. M interrogates him, and while doing so he tries to assassinate M with a cyanide pistol. As the story unravels, we find that Bond had made his way to Russia, where the KGB brainwashed him.

Upon deprogramming, Bond wishes to recover his double-O status, and so is sent on a mission to Jamaica to find and infiltrate the web surrounding Fransisco Scaramanga, an assassin who has been killing secret service operatives. Scaramanga is known as the man with the golden gun because of his golden .45 revolver. Bond succeeds in discovering that there is a much wider syndicate in operation involving the KGB and gangsters, and with the help of Felix Leiter and Bond girl Mary Goodnight, Scaramanga and his helpers are all killed.

We are for the first time given M's real name: Sir Miles Messervy, which means "ill-treated brother." We are also told that Bond is offered a knighthood, which he turns down. Did Fleming hope to gain a knighthood himself? Was he the ill-treated brother? We can only wonder.

►◄

This chapter was intended only as a brief outline of the various Bond novels. The tales in *Octopussy and the Living Daylights*, the final Fleming collection of short stories, occur between the various novels.

Bond began *Thunderball* in disgrace and poor health, and in *On Her Majesty's Secret Service* he is growing weary. In *You Only Live Twice* he is torn apart by the death of his wife, and in all he is still searching for something—a lonely, empty character, trying desperately to fulfil something in his life. The misery of the creator, Fleming, is played out on the pages, and the full weight of his esoteric knowledge and game-playing is brought to bear in order for him to try and understand himself. As Fleming said to his wife, Anne, "How can I make you happy, when I am so miserable myself?"[2]

We have seen briefly that there are small glimpses of etymological and plot code laid out before us in Fleming's novels, and that he seemed to understand the use of language and numerology as code. In order to begin to comprehend the influences from which Fleming received the knowledge to include this almost subconscious self-analysis, we need to look at the man's life in more detail.

CHAPTER 3

IAN FLEMING, PART II: EARLY INFLUENCES

From the very start it appears that Ian Fleming was doomed to suffer the effects of an overbearing and dominating mother, an elder brother who managed to succeed in everything he did, and a heroic and highly successful deceased father.

His mother's family was of royal blood, and her name has implications of Rosicrucianism (Brethren of the Rose and Cross)—the cross and the rose, or St. Croix-Rose. The royal connections seemed to help, as in 1925 Mrs. Fleming's illegitimate daughter, Ian's half-sister, Amaryllis (1925–1999), was born in Switzerland with the aid of Viscount Dawson of Penn, with Princess Marie Louise becoming her godmother. Marie Louise was a member of the British royal family, and granddaughter of Queen Victoria.

Ian's father had inherited Robert Fleming's immense banking operations, known as Robert Fleming and Co., which were finally sold to Chase Manhattan Bank in 2000 for $7 billion.

The overall truth of the matter was that Ian Fleming had nothing to worry about. His mother had inherited a vast estate, albeit tied to her never marrying again, but that didn't stop her from having a child out of wedlock. The influences that the old Scottish Fleming family had were large and wide, with friends not just within the ranks of the royal families, but also in business and parliament. Winston Churchill, the wartime prime minister, was just one such friend.

Sir Winston Churchill

This was the world into which little Ian Fleming was born and was to grow—a small child looking to his one parent for love and affection, and finding a nanny and a focused, achieving brother instead. He was given the very best of everything, and lacked the one thing a child really needs: the love of his parents. His mother was all too often busy with her various socialite roles, and, regardless of the fact that Ian Fleming himself didn't leave us a day-by-day account of his childhood, it does not take a top-class psychologist to work out that he would have had issues from this alone.

In addition, the influences surrounding him were not normal. Not every child is brought up in a household frequented by peers of the realm, listening at the door to the gossip of royals and the late-night maneuverings of Evelyn's lover, Augustus John the painter. I was brought up in a typical British family home, where both my mother and father worked, but were still somehow always there for us. I had a standard education in a standard school, and knew the love of my family. And yet, my own children answer the phone to speak to well-known personalities whom I know, and see their father on the TV screen and hear him on radio. I can see how this small amount of unusualness affects them in minor ways. How much more would we be affected if we were raised in the same manner as Ian Fleming?

The fact is that Ian Fleming was trouble. He rebelled internally and externally, and tried desperately to overcome a great many issues created by a great many influences. At school he failed his expectant mother, who moved him around like a royal pawn.

In 1927, Ian Fleming was packed off to Kitzbuhel in Austria to spend time with the Forbes Dennises—followers of the supposedly new form of psychology brought about by Alfred Adler, very much in the same time frame as Carl Jung and Sigmund Freud.

Alfred Adler, who inspired Forbes Dennis

Forbes Dennis was one of the closest admirers of the Adlerian psychoanalysis. He argued that the human personality could be explained as a battle between the self-ideal, what we truly desired, and the social and ethical demands of the world around us. He said that if the issues caused by this were not corrected, then the individual would overcompensate, creating inferiority complexes, and resulting in the individual becoming egocentric, power-hungry, and aggressive. It is easy to see why Ian Fleming was sent to Dennis, as these were the traits he had developed. Dennis was to say later that, on the surface, Fleming was "more difficult than ever," being rude, resentful, and determined to make the most out of his own disgrace. And yet beneath the surface he was bored and disappointed, like "a weathercock," as his varying moods chased each other around. One of Dennis's pupils would later state that Fleming was "like someone straight out of a novel, and he seemed the living proof of all her Adlerian theories."[1]

Adler believed that many psychological problems were derived from the birth order, or the placing of siblings within the family. He observed that the firstborn child would be loved and nurtured by the family until the second child arrived, at which point the firstborn would suffer from dethronement, and no longer be the center of all attention. There has, however, since this revelation, been no scientific support, and Adler himself couldn't produce evidence to prove his case, which is quite the opposite of what happened with the Flemings. Peter Fleming was the elder brother, and he, quite to the contrary of Adler's assumptions, succeeded, and Ian Fleming, the younger child, did not, until much later in life. But there was more to the Adler theories.

He believed that the first five years of a child's life were the most important. His theory revolved around the *Gegenspieler*—the contemporary brother or sister with whom there is a seemingly endless neurotic duel.

The Gegenspieler may have been the parent or contemporary brother or sister by whom the individual would feel dethroned or placed at a distance. The danger in this situation, according to Phyllis Bottome, was in the very fact that the individual was unconscious of the effect, and that it would affect the future relationships as the child developed into adult-hood, creating a perpetual antagonism between the individual and any loved ones.[2]

As this perpetual antagonism continues, argued Adler, the individual gradually moved further and further away from reality and into the powerful world of the unconscious. This neurotic individual lived a life of fantasy and imagination, employing various devices to allow him to circumvent reality. He fixated on an imagined ideal in order to free himself from his own feelings of inferiority, and gain absolution from all responsibility. If ever there were a true statement about the mind of Ian Fleming in his childhood (and later in his life, to a somewhat lesser degree), then this is it.

Adler stated that the cure for this neurosis was to change the whole upbringing of the individual and guide him back into society. Unfortunately for Ian Fleming, it was too late, and all Dennis and his cohort Bottome could do was supply large quantities of encouragement and love—something he had sadly lacked in his childhood. It is a fact that Ian Fleming understood the process in which he was placed, and understood the great affection shown to him while in Austria.

In his book *Thrilling Cities*, Ian Fleming wrote: "I remember in those days before the war, reading, thanks to the encouragement of the Forbes Dennises, the works of Kafka, Musil, the Zweigs, Arthur Schintzler, Werfel, Rilke, von Hofmannsthal, and those bizarre psychologists Weininger and Groddeck—let alone the writings of Adler and Freud—and buying the first editions (I used to collect them) illustrated Kokoschka and Kubin."

This one statement reveals a number of things. Firstly, that Fleming understood the psychological process and therefore comprehended his own shortcomings. It also reveals his wide knowledge of the new world of psychoanalysis. Finally, it reveals that the whole affair was still very much on his mind many years later.

It seems, however, that the work of the Dennises had paid off as Fleming's confidence grew. As Fleming reached the age of 19, Dennis himself said that Fleming's qualities were considerable, with a general intelligence well above average. He claimed that the young man was possessed of imagination, originality, and the power of self-expression, having built an excellent taste of books and a strong desire for truth and knowledge. "He is virile and ambitious; generous and kind-hearted.... He requires time to handle a complex personality."[3]

We see here at this early age that Fleming had a "definite desire for both truth and knowledge," as Forbes Dennis said. These are profound statements from a man who understood the workings of the mind. Fleming may have been aggressive, hard-headed, and obstinate, but he was also generous and kind-hearted. The statement reveals a distinct split personality that would stay with Fleming for the rest of his life.

It seems that Fleming also had a way with the girls, and boosted his self-confidence by flirting and conquering. Like so many other writers, fables, and myths before and since, he even associated sex with the divided nation in which he was raised: "Technique in bed is important, but alone it is the scornful coupling that makes the affairs of Austrians and Anglo-Saxons so fragmentary and in the end distasteful."[4]

Fleming had learned that true male-female connection in both the mind and the body was reconnection to a higher cause, and so he romanticized it. This was the beginning of the Bond-girl role he would build into the success of the nation's greatest spy.

He began to cut out a role for himself that he would later flesh out in Bond, and which would split in time into many facets of his own mind. While with the Forbes Dennises at Tennerhof he would play the correct individual and fit in with the regime, but down at the Café Reisch he played the amorous lover, swimming and skiing, climbing and making love. Both groups would see a completely different Fleming. He was developing his split personalities, not curing the problem. He was becoming a master of disguise without a mask.

Lady Sackville

But all along he was completely conscious of what he was doing. Fleming hinted at his own concept of his inner balance in a letter to Lady Sackville at Knole—a well-married Gypsy with whom Fleming found solace:

I am much too apt to be affected by externals. They force themselves so much upon one that it is difficult to ignore them unless one is a hermit or a fanatic of some sort, in which case one is generally a large brain with a tiny little forgotten body attached. But when one is fairly equal parts brain and body—as I am—neither half is strong enough to exclude the other, so consequently at least half my life is made up of externals, which always try their best to intrude on my poor other half—however, it's better than extremes in either direction.[5]

We can see in these personal letters hints at his knowledge of his own divided mind. Fleming knew from the copious books he read and lessons he learned that he was a troubled man, and so he corrected this later in the world of fantasy, by placing himself as the perfect man in the pages of the Bond books. At this early stage in his development, he did attempt to live out his fantasy world in ideas. He never wrote down these ideas, but he did have a great many theories about a novel he would one day write. He wrote of them in letters to his good friend Selby Armitage in London. However, whatever it was that these letters truly contained, they were so abhorrent to the elder Ian Fleming that he asked for them back from Armitage, and destroyed them utterly. No trace of these letters has ever been found.

What was it in these letters that so embarrassed Fleming? One can only now guess, and mine would be that they all too clearly outlined his troubles.

▶◀

Fleming moved on from Kitzbuhel to Geneva University. Here he collected first editions of Kokoschka and Picasso, and even spoke to Einstein, who greatly impressed him, at the League of Nations. But the most telling of things also occurred: Through the permission granted by Jung himself via Forbes Dennis, he translated a lecture given by Jung on the infamous alchemist, philosopher, and (some say) scientist, Paracelsus.

Although Fleming never spoke publicly about why this particular lecture had caught his eye, and it was never published, he nevertheless showed it to Dame Edith Sitwell some years later, and they even considered writing a joint book on the subject.

Carl Gustav Jung, the infamous psychologist

I would submit that Fleming did indeed have a good motive to translate this lecture, and it is the very underlying reasons for this book. Fleming understood what Jung and Paracelsus were about, because their theories resonated within his own mind. However, in order for us to understand what so intrigued Fleming, we must understand who Paracelsus was, and delve into this previously unpublished and relatively unknown translation of Jung's lecture.

CHAPTER 4

PARACELSUS AND GNOSIS

Theophrastus Philippus Aureolus Bombastus von Hohenheim, born on November 11, 1493, in Einsiedeln, Switzerland, later took the name Paracelsus, meaning "beside/better than or similar to Celsus," the Roman physician of the first century AD. His father was a chemist, and as a youth he worked as an analyst at nearby mines. At the tender age of 16 he began studying medicine at Basel University, and then later at Vienna, gaining a doctorate from the University of Ferrara. At the time, chemistry and alchemy were little different, and in fact were both seen as the search for ultimate truth and the science of nature. In the search for these truths, Paracelsus traveled extensively, visiting Egypt, Arabia, the Holy Land, and Constantinople. He brought back to Europe a wealth of knowledge, including medical treatments, from the enlightened medieval Islamic world, which would bring him fame. On the face of it, Paracelsus rejected

Gnostic traditions, instead leaning towards Hermetic, Pythagorean, and neoplatonic philosophies. However, many scholars believe that his supposed rejection of Gnostic philosophies was not substantiated due to his Aristotelian Hermetical reasonings. The truth of the matter is simple: It was the magical elements of Agrippa and Flamel that Paracelsus was not in agreement with—seeing them as unreal, even though he was a practicing astrologer. There is a little contradiction in this reasoning, for Paracelsus devoted several chapters in his book *Archidoxes of Magic* to talismans for various maladies according to the signs of the Zodiac—a very magical thing to do. He also invented an alphabet for the Magi, used

Paracelsus

for engraving angelic names upon talismans. Later on, following being virtually chased from Basel, he wandered the streets of Europe, Africa, and Asia Minor in the search for hidden knowledge.

Psychoanalyst Carl Gustav Jung lectured on Paracelsus because he had uncovered the secrets of psychology from ancient sources, and it was to this that Fleming was drawn—seeing it as a route to his own inner salvation. I believe Fleming would have been at home with Paracelsus's motto: "Let no man belong to another that can belong to himself."

Indeed Fleming would also have been impressed with Paracelsus's *Spagyrical Writings*: "From time immemorial artistic insights have been revealed to artists in their sleep and dreams, so that at all times they ardently desired them. Then their imagination could work wonders upon wonders and invoke the shades of the philosophies, who would instruct them in their art."[1]

Indeed, I believe it was the shades of these philosophers that Fleming would invoke in his writing. We have to understand that in Fleming's youth, alchemy was seen as nothing more than the forerunner of chemistry, and anything else was simply superstitious nonsense. It is only today that alchemy is once again being seen for what it truly was—much more than just a forerunner of chemistry. In fact, alchemy is little different from Gnosticism in that it is a work upon the self; the varying methods of self-improvement and psychology leading to the realization of the true self, which was termed the divine in the self. Often this would involve a mystical experience and a feeling of oneness with the universe or deity, and a sense of all-knowledge. In this union of the dual natures of the mind, early psychoanalysts such as Jung saw an ancient method that may indeed work—balance. And it is for this reason that Paracelsus could not have detested Gnosticism, for balance is at the root of it. Indeed, Gnosticism was the first love of Jung, and his dedication to its systems was relentless. In fact, I too feel very much the same way, which is why I wrote *Gnosis: The Secret of Solomon's Temple Revealed*, to show to people that there are methods, as old as man, to aid in our own regeneration and self-worth.

To understand what is meant by the term *gnosis*, we must understand the same point that Jung tried to make to Freud: that the wisdom of what the Gnostics called *Sophia* must rise within us. Sophia is the feminine principal within our own psyche, and in this way she is worshipped as a goddess. It was the love of this Sophia, or wisdom, that gave rise to the term *philosopher*—a lover of wisdom. The male and often dominating part of ourselves was all too often the fiery and arrogant self. United, the powerful male-oriented side and the wise feminine principle would fuse within us to create the son of the divine. The trouble for people such as Jung (and he was the leading light) was that Gnosticism seemed ancient in the early 20th century, and the link to the past appeared to have been broken. However, through Jung's tenacious spirit he adventured into the world of alchemy and discovered that it was the carrier of this ancient wisdom. The truth was that Gnosticism had been silenced by the Church of Rome, even though later finds at Nag Hammadi would prove that Christianity had been spawned from within the very folds of Gnostic lore. And so the truth of our very selves was hidden from us so that mankind would have to go through an intercessor such as the priest in order to control his own urges and improve his time on earth. All the time the Church grew in power and wealth, and Europe slipped into the Dark Ages. But in the Middle East and in Asia Minor, as Jung and Paracelsus would later discover, there was a wealth of wisdom literature and wisdom teachers.

While Europe hacked off infected legs, our friends on distant shores healed them. While Europe tied ropes around the necks of unbelievers, in far-off lands alchemy and psychology were fostered. When the two cultures clashed, bastions of knowledge such as the Library of Alexandria were burned to the ground, and the people kept in the dark. But beneath the cloak of this dark history crept a wise serpent, feeding knowledge, gnosis, and wisdom into secretive orders and alchemical texts. These, in fact, were the true treasures brought back to Europe by the orders such as the Knights Templar. Many would have us believe that these treasures were variously the Holy Grail, the Ark of the Covenant, or even the head of Christ, and in a symbolic or metaphysical way this would be true, but in the physical sense it is not so. It is true that treasures were created and relics made and then sold on the mass Christian market, but alas, the real treasure was hidden within alchemical texts, structures of sacred geometry, and art of divine proportions—all revealing where God truly resided. This true place the Gnostics knew to be at the fusion point within the mind. There erupted in the Middle Ages and medieval periods great storytelling that on the surface appeared to be nothing more than religious or state propaganda. However, slithering, hidden from site, was the wise serpent of the Gnostics.

King Arthur

One such tale is still to this day almost as popular as ever—multi-million-dollar films are made of the tale of King Arthur, the Holy Grail, and Arthur's wife Guinevere. This tale has at its heart the truth of gnosis, and most people completely miss it.

King Arthur is the hero of the tale. He is strong and forceful, but not overly wise. He is the heir to the throne of the land, as we are heirs to our own soul. ("Let no man belong to another that can belong to himself.")

The land is troubled; it is overrun by invaders (or externals), who need eradicating or bringing into control. But Arthur needs a queen to help rule the land. He already has the mighty and powerful serpent-adorned sword, but needs the softening charms of wisdom to wield it. Guinevere will be his queen, as the queen of serpents herself, married to the head dragon (Pendragon) of Arthur. The serpent is consistently found in Gnostic literature and alchemical works, and the tales of Arthur are alchemical and Gnostic tales, slipped under the radar of the Catholic authorities. They speak about a mind needing balance, and they are a warning to us all, for when Arthur and Guinevere are divided, just like the divided mind, the land becomes infertile, and so too does the mind of man become useless when in a state of duality. In this way Ian Fleming slipped beneath the cloak of fiction the subtle serpent of balance and wisdom. As we have seen in previous chapters, the dragon or serpent is used within the Bond tales as both a positive and negative force, just as Fleming found in the ancient tales, and this place of balance is termed the neutral state. Ian Fleming himself said of James Bond, "Exotic things would happen to and around him but he would be a neutral figure...."[2]

The alchemical *Rosarium Philosophorum* (Rosary of the Philosophers) was used extensively by Jung to express this divine union of opposites. In the text there are 10 pictures illustrating the great work (opus) of alchemical transformation, and these reveal the king and queen undergoing a number of transitions in a mystical and erotic way. Eventually they are transformed into a new hermaphrodite, or androgynous being, called the Nobel Empress. In the images, the lovers meet first clothed and then unclothed, symbolizing the purity of their connection. They are confronting each other with truth and in truth. Next they are immersed in the alchemical bath, submerging to remove their falseness, and in *conjunction*, or union, and this results in death, from which the pure spirit or consciousness rises reborn like the phoenix. This new being is neither the king nor the queen, but a re-creation of the true self, ultimately united.

This was the world in which Ian Fleming found himself. This is the creeping serpent of which Fleming saw much more than glimpses in the work of Carl Jung and Paracelsus, and this would be the message he would underpin in his Bond novels and other work. Bond would become Arthur, and he would only succeed in union with the feminine principle. But Jung had already done the hard work for us all, he had already sifted through the many ancient texts, and Fleming, as a divided man, eagerly followed. Jung said: "First I had to find evidence for the historical prefiguration of my own inner experiences. That is to say, I had to ask myself, 'Where have my particular premises already occurred in history?' If I had not succeeded in finding such evidence, I would never have been able to substantiate my ideas. There, my encounter with alchemy was decisive for me, as it provided me with the historical basis which I hitherto lacked."[3]

><

Jung pointed out the redemptive aspects of the works of Paracelsus, and it must have been this element to which Fleming was drawn.

Paracelsus pointed out that human alchemists are capable of inducing the process of change or transformation, which will liberate the light of the divine held captive by the physical form. This was what Fleming needed, and in many respects used as an excuse for his own failings—his physical form locked in the light.

Jung found himself in a world of 16th- and 17th-century alchemists, and discovered that it "represented a link with Gnosticism" and that a "continuity therefore existed between past and present. Grounded in the natural philosophy of the Middle Ages, alchemy formed the bridge on the one hand into the past, to Gnosticism, and on the other into the future, to the modern psychology of the unconscious."[4]

Alchemy

Fleming too would read original texts, buying many for his collection, and he too would discover that one of England's leading alchemists under Queen Elizabeth I would become a pattern for Fleming's alternate ego to follow—Dr. John Dee. There shall be more on this element later; for now we need to understand what it was about alchemy that firstly relates to psychology, and secondly that relates to Fleming's James Bond.

In the first place, alchemy, as the work upon the self, involves looking into the mirror at ourselves—into our inner selves. What we find when we do so is not always pretty. In fact, it can be quite ugly. This is why alchemy speaks of reducing and burning. It is not always about reducing the base substance of lead into its prime material, and then by magical or chemical means creating gold—an element that often figures in the Bond novels. Instead it is about reducing the rubbish, chaff, dross (call it what you will) of our own lives, to reveal what was there at the beginning—the soul of man. Does not Bond in each book suffer the torment of this reduction? Is he not tortured before he can then reunite and be reborn? It is one of the prime plot levels of each book, as we have seen.

Once this process has been performed, we discover that it is an ongoing process that must be repeated again and again, just as each Bond book reveals. The reason is simple: The "externals" of the world are a

Queen Elizabeth I

strong force upon the mind. As Fleming said: "I am much too apt to be affected by externals. They force themselves so much upon one...."

These "externals" are influences from our peers, from the press, from friends, relatives, and colleagues. They are pressures that arise because of the world system in which we function, and if we are not to lose our own humanity—our souls—then we must constantly use reductionism and burn off the negative influences that affect us. In this way the mind of Fleming would struggle with the influences of the world, because he was very much part of the system and driven by the creative desire to impress his mother and his dead father, and to be as good as, if not better than, his big brother, Peter. Eventually it seems that Fleming grew so accustomed to this inner battle that he befriended it, and instead of working upon himself, he worked out his battles on the pages of the Bond novels.

This mind had been formed from influences gained while with the Dennises in Austria. They had been steered by his reading and understanding of very ancient truths, and by the mind of Carl Jung, who had given Fleming permission to translate his lecture on Paracelsus. It is to this lecture that we must now turn in order to understand Fleming's creations more deeply.

CHAPTER 5

THE LECTURE

Having discovered that the creator of James Bond had actually attended lectures by Carl Jung, and that he had even translated one on Paracelsus, I was intrigued to read the lecture for myself. I presumed wrongly that the lecture would have been well-known. A man as infamous as Ian Fleming would surely have had every part and detail of his life laid bare for all to see, but I was wrong. In fact, I was amazed that I was discovering elements of Fleming's personality that were either not known, or not spoken of. I was sure that this text, so loved by Fleming that he wished to translate it, would give me an insight into the formulating mind of the spy novelist.

First we need to look into the mind of Carl Jung in order to discover what it was about this man that so fascinated Ian Fleming.

Carl Jung

*At the primitive stage, the need to surround ourselves in mystery is of the vital importance, and the shared secret is the **bond** which holds the group together. At the social level, secrecy is a necessary compensation for the lack of cohesion in the individual's personality which, after constant relapses into the unconscious original identity shared with others, is always breaking up and scattering again. An apologia for secrecy.*

—Carl Jung, *My Life*

Born on June 26, 1875, Carl Jung was one of the most famous and infamous psychiatrists the world has ever known. He founded analytical psychiatry, and emphasized the understanding of the psyche—the mind—through the exploration of dreams, mythology, art, philosophy, and religion. He practiced his trade for much of his life, while developing his own unique insights, often at odds with the established and staid world of psychiatry. Jung delved deeply into the world of the occult, alchemy, astrology, literature, and art, and came away with an overriding sense that what man needed was balance and harmony.

Before the middle of the 20th century, the words *alchemy* and *gnosis* were little mentioned other than in the circles of the secret societies and those interested in the occult. But Jung changed all this, and brought the arcane and sacred teachings of our ancestors into the forefront. Before he published his thoughts on alchemy, those people who had heard of the word simply ascribed it to the ancient techniques of chemistry, as many alchemists did discover new chemicals and provide the world with some amazing new medicines. However, this was not the root of the system, as Jung would discover. Without his input, the world of the alchemist would probably remain the world of the occult, but Jung brought this ancient teaching into the view of the modern world, and today it is discussed on many levels. However, Jung's first and last love was for Gnosticism. In 1912 he wrote to Sigmund Freud, stating that the wisdom of the Gnostics, namely Sophia, would one day soon reenter the Western culture by way of a new form of psychology.

But for this lone researcher, life was not easy. Back in the early part of the 20th century there weren't copious books on Gnostic history or beliefs, so Jung had to dedicate a vast amount of time and resources to getting hold of original texts and translations. Throughout the years Jung accumulated a knowledge base, and reformulated in a modern way what the Gnostics had been saying. We saw in the previous chapter the understanding that Jung came to, and that he was highly influenced by Paracelsus, but he was also influenced by other great luminaries in the Gnostic creed: people such as the heretical Irenaeus and Hippolytus, and the alchemically aligned Valentius and Basilides.

Today we have an ongoing translation of the infamous Nag Hammadi texts to help us, but Jung had to gather his knowledge from texts such as the *Pistis Sophia*, contemporaneously translated by George Mead. Jung was so fascinated by this translation that he actually tracked Mead down to London in order to express his gratitude.

One thing continued to crop up in his research—the link between the early Gnostics of 2,000 years ago and those today. Where was the thread of Gnostic thought in modern times? Had it died out completely? Or had it transformed? Jung was one of the very first men to discover this thread to be alchemy. In simple terms, the beliefs of the Gnostics—that the divine is within ourselves and that we need to be perfectly balanced in order to access, understand, and grow with this—were no different from the analogies and metaphors found within the texts, myths, and art of the medieval alchemists, and that this must therefore be the continuation of gnosis.

Sigmund Freud

But Jung was fighting an established tide, and the master of this tide seemed to be his old friend Sigmund Freud. In 1914, Herbert Silberer, a disciple of Freud, published a work that dealt with the psychoanalytical implications of alchemy. Freud utterly rebuked Silberer, who then committed suicide. It seemed that if Jung were to open up his own ideas and concepts on alchemy, then he too would have to deal with the wrath of Freud. But Jung knew his own mind, and knew that he could not be held back by the concept of Master that Silberer so obviously placed upon Freud. What Jung did was to build up his knowledge base in order to further his belief and prove his case. He also made it abundantly clear in his later writings that he was well aware that this new understanding would distance him from Freud, and he hoped that it would not mean the loss of a friend. Letters between Jung and Freud, however, do prove that the distance grew into a wide and insurmountable gulf.

By 1930, Jung had discovered from the word of the German sinologist, Richard Wilhelm, that the Chinese had for many centuries also practiced and understood what the West call Gnosticism in their very own version of alchemy. In fact, Jung discovered that there was little difference at all between East and West in the concept that the agonies of life as a human arose from the knowledge of the human soul—of our own consciousness. This confrontation with the truth of our very existence, of birth and death, gave rise to the spiritual and alchemical union of opposites often termed the lunar queen and solar king, and well known in China as the yin and yang.

The Gnosis of Sophia

With the advent of books in the genre of *The Da Vinci Code*, much of the world seems to have awakened to the idea of the feminine principle or Mother Goddess via the sacred union of Christ and Mary Magdalene, precisely as Carl Jung predicted. However, there were a great many people who were already aware of this aspect of our past, but not in the literal sense, and it is the search for the truth of this hidden past that we seek now. For the seeking of the truth shall reveal that the so-called Da Vinci Code was not a literal concept—Jesus did not literally unite with Mary—but a literary code, the light of the sun uniting with the goddess of the moon.

Throughout the course of generations the wisdom of the feminine principle was covered up by the Church and made masculine—eroding thousands of years of balance, and tipping it towards a male-dominated theology against which Carl Jung vehemently spoke out. But the cover-up was not strong enough, and now, in today's environment of free speech and lack of fear of the Church, we can once again unleash the power of wisdom that is truly the Sophia of the Gnostics.

Gnosis is derived from a Greek word, and means "knowledge." But the English language has always failed in the interpretation of foreign words, especially those of ancient languages. In truth, *gnosis* means the "mystical experience of the Divine in the Self." It is a concept that our historians tell us gave rise to many of the beliefs in Christianity, which were then picked over for the mainstream theology. Deep in the heart of Gnostic belief was the goddess Sophia, and it is this wisdom that is derived from the mystical experience of the Divine in the Self. She is at the heart of our deepest and most natural core; she is the intuitive state—the connection to the greater universe and nature itself. This is not a New Age concept made fun of by ordinary society, but is in fact something to be found at the very center of all the world's religions, if only we take the time to seek her out.

Take Solomon's Temple for instance. What we find is that this temple is in the form of man (and woman). It is laid out to sacred geometrical proportions upon the ground. It is in essence the Divine, as man in time (tempos), and therefore brings heaven to earth so that we can connect to the Divinity in balance and harmony. But what are these words, *balance* and *harmony*, if the temple is simply to a male god? Well, it was not and is not simply a male-dominated temple, and all the evidence is there awaiting us, like a treasure chest full of riches we cannot imagine.

To understand, we must take a brief look at the Canaanite-Phoenician goddess Asherah. She is known by many names, such as "she who treads on water" or "the Holy One." These are remarkable statements, especially as it was the "Christ" or enlightened one who was to walk on water, and who was the Holy One. In Sumeria, Asherah is called Ashratum, and is the bride of Anu, the Shining One. She is the moon to his sun, and they work in perfect balance and harmony, as we must if we are to have gnosis or true knowledge of the Divine—for the true Divine is not male, nor female, but balance between them. In the Israelite religion, Asherah is also known as Shekinah, and is married with Yahweh—a fact later blotted out by Judaism and Christianity. She is also known as Dat ba'thani or the Lady of the Serpent, revealing another symbol also vilified—the snake—and a symbol that we find used quite often by Fleming in his Bond novels.

Throughout time and across the world the serpent was worshiped as a symbol of the duality, energy, power, and wisdom of man. It was good and bad, positive and negative, male and female. It speaks of enlightenment and gives knowledge to Eve (meaning "female serpent," from *hawwah*). But it was made evil, as the feminine principle was demonized, and hundreds of years later we have a male-dominated, warlike world that lacks the balance of the feminine principle of wisdom. Let me explain in the same way that the Bible explained it.

Solomon (male side of ourselves) was the king of Israel. He was powerful and vengeful (similar to Yahweh). He was so arrogant that he asked, "Who is there in the whole world that does not know of my fame?" In answer to this the hoopoe bird replied that there was one, and she was the Queen of Sheba (Saba)—the Queen of Serpents (the feminine, wise side of ourselves). This hoopoe bird is the element of our own mind known as the internal dialog, where we converse with ourselves. It was the mind telling the positive-male-dominated side that there was another element that he should listen to, the negative-female-principle. Negative is not a derisive word in this context, it is simply opposite. In fact, this feminine principle is wisdom or water to the fire. The element of water is always female, and this is why the word is linked in etymology to Mary, who is symbolized with a boat in a great many places. So too are Isis, Ishtar, and others. These two opposites need to fuse together if the person is to be fully formed and in balance. Solomon and Sheba come together, and the temple is complete and wholly formed. When they once again divide, Israel falls apart and the tribes disperse; the Ark (connection to the Divine) goes missing from the Holy of Holies (the mind), and so we must await the coming-together-again.

The female serpent of wisdom was in the temple as Asherah poles—large wooden poles entwined with serpents—but alas, even these were turned masculine by calling them Asher*im* (the masculine word-ending in Hebrew). These poles were caduceus-like, a tree entwined with two serpents in balance, known as the Tree of Life and Knowledge.

The knowledge of this sacred union did not completely die out, though, as Jung discovered. During Europe's Dark Ages the Middle East kept Sophia alive, and following the later Crusades, a great many secrets were brought back to Europe under the very eyes of the Catholic Church. Much of this newfound knowledge can still be seen in our modern world in buildings, art, and language. Algebra, medicine, and architecture are the most obvious, but *gnosis* is the underlying and more dangerous aspect that seeped back into Europe via orders such as the Knights Templar and the Cistercians. The knowledge of Gnosis was understood, but was directly in opposition to the manipulating propaganda of the male-oriented mainstream Church, so it went underground. Today we can find these truths in the very stories populated by the orders of the Templars and Cistercians—such as the tales of the Holy Grail and Arthurian fables. Arthur Pendragon, the head (pen) serpent (dragon) is married to Guinevere (the queen of serpents), and as they are united the land is fertile, and all is good. As they are "lanced" apart, the land becomes infertile, and evil sets in. There is little difference here from the tale of Solomon and Sheba, and we can also find this in stories of Robin and Marion and a great many more.

With new eyes we can now see truths about our very selves left in stories. We can see a wonderful system of psychology set in a spiritual context. We must not be divided within our own minds, but must be in balance. We must control the fiery male-oriented aspect with the feminine balance of wisdom. Control of the power and wisdom within our minds is derived from true gnosis, and via the mystical experience or enlightenment we can become conscious of this.

This is the wisdom that Carl Jung intuitively understood, and from his own inner experiences sought out in the world of myth and alchemy.

It was to Paracelsus that Jung turned as a tool to offer up an analogy of himself—as the man who struggled with the contempt of his peers in order to bring true wisdom into the world and it was this very lecture that Ian Fleming was so influenced by at a very early age.

The Lecture

I searched the Internet for the text, and found that there were virtually no mentions of the lecture at all, let alone a transcript of it. I was surprised. It took me some time, but eventually I found that the translation had been given to Dame Edith Sitwell as a gift. I tracked down the estate of Sitwell to find that many of her papers were now in the hands of the Harry Ransom Center at the University of Texas at Austin. I jumped at this immediately and contacted the center, asking for permission to firstly see the text, and then to use it. I was granted both, and the following is an analysis of the remarkable translation of Paracelsus: A Speech, held at his birthplace, the Devil's Bridge, Einsiedeln, June 22, 1929, by Carl Gustav Jung (then translated from German by I.L. Fleming).

The lecture begins simply outlining the birth of Paracelsus in 1493, placing his birth in the sign of the scorpion—a favorable omen for healers, poisoners, and physicians. It then moves on to something of which we spoke in the last chapter—the understanding and metaphor of the divine balance. We are told by Jung that Father Sun and Mother Earth were the forgers of the character of Paracelsus, more so than by his blood.

There is also discussion of the fact that Paracelsus's own grandfather was of the Order of St. John and born within the magic circle of the

Alps, and I think that a lot of the heritage of Paracelsus must have resonated with Fleming, as did the statement that his father was a gloomy,
solitary figure with noble blood, and that "[n]o spiritual consideration
works more strongly upon the human environment, especially of the
child, than the unexperienced life of the parents."

Jung pointed out that we could expect to find a profound influence
from the parents upon the young Paracelsus. The tragedy of the life of
Paracelsus, we are told, will be that he will spend his life trying to *be* his
father, and improve his father's standing through his own actions, and
thereby lose all true connection to his friends. I think we can see that
this resonated well with Fleming, and that the fantastic globe-trotting
adventures of his 16th-century hero would formulate in his mind—as
did the scandalous way that Paracelsus would not follow the norm.

Jung then makes a statement that goes completely against the pro-
fessed belief of Paracelsus himself. We are told that at the age of 38 a
metamorphosis occurred, and suddenly the medical man turned into a
philosophical man, but Jung says quite plainly that this term, *philosophic*,
is incorrect, for what Paracelsus was revealing was the Gnostic man.
This is precisely what I recognized in the tales of James Bond from the
start. Both Jung and Fleming recognized this Gnostic element, and both
would spend their lives trying to firstly understand it, and secondly use
it as a tool for self-improvement. Jung tells us that this change occurred
in Paracelsus in his mid-life, and that it is a common spiritual occur-
rence, something we probably call (incorrectly) today the "midlife cri-
sis." This element occurs "in the subliminal self." Indeed, we can see
from the original manuscript of the translation that Fleming tried to
understand this concept, for his initial translation was "before the threshold of the unconscious," and then he writes in pencil by hand "in the

subliminal self." This reveals his desire to get the lecture translation right, as well as his understanding that his first attempt at this statement wasn't. Indeed, this element is not "before the threshold of the unconscious," as this is a state of physical action, and is instead something just below consciousness—in other words, subliminal.

We are then told by Jung that Paracelsus died a good Catholic, and that he simply dealt with his own inner and occult thought by placing his intellect in one drawer and his conscience in another. Fleming would also do the same with his life, and thereby avoid friction.

Jung then tells us of the *hyaster*, a hybrid word from *hyle*, or "matter," and *astrum*, or "cosmic." It is the cosmic matter, the union of that which is above, with that which is below—the forming of force and matter. It is revealed in the *limbus*, a large circle for the spiritually animated world and a smaller circle for the man, demonstrating that whatever is outside, is also inside and vice versa. The world of the material was animated by the same force as the spiritual world, and Jung predicts that we will yet be amazed that we could have forgotten such ancient truths. This force, the correspondence between the material and spiritual worlds, he calls *entia*. Maladies could be cured by using *entia* against *entia*, spirit upon spirit.

The concepts of medicine for the body and medicine for the mind and soul discussed by Jung in the lecture reveal the ancient wisdom of gnosis. For Jung there was no separation between the theories and beliefs of Paracelsus and the ancient concepts of gnosis. He was the obstinate proponent of healing the self, and this was for too long an occult or hidden legacy, both hidden and lost by the Church that was supposed to guide the people. Paracelsus suffered badly at the hands of his fellow physicians, as Fleming was to suffer at the hands of his contemporary critics, and yet both have grown beyond all those opponents. Paracelsus lead the way with his cures and his philosophic beliefs, and maybe he found them because he needed them. It is a distinct truth that a great many people become healers because they need healing, and Fleming too would come to the ancient truths of gnosis, seen here clearly in his own hand and typeface, because he was in serious need of healing inside.

►◄

Fleming would take all that he was learning and begin to formulate his own method of storytelling. He would create his own modern-day King Arthur, and whether consciously or subconsciously (subliminal), he would bring all these influences together, squeezed into the tightly spun stories of James Bond.

Jung's lectures and other works inspired Fleming in a deeper, psychological world—a world of light and darkness that spoke to Fleming's inner experiences. The *lumen naturae*, or the light or force of nature, spoken of by the alchemists and pointed out by Jung in his lecture on Paracelsus and alchemy, would rise in the *Hildebrand Rarity* of Ian Fleming, the lunar queen and solar king would unite in the repetitive tales of James Bond and his feminine counterparts, and the darkness that resides within and must be overcome would find fruition in the constant nemesis with which Bond would struggle.

To our modern minds, the world of Jung, Paracelsus, gnosis, and alchemy seems strange and far removed from our everyday, practical lives. And this is the beauty of the whole thing—that complexity of word, symbol, code, and cipher, hides a simple understanding. So simple that it had to be hidden. True spirituality, true wisdom and understanding will be found within the true self, if only we can discover what this is. When we go to the movies and watch a James Bond film, a large percentage of us will emerge with a subconscious (and sometimes conscious) desire to *be* James Bond. We will wish to buy a fast, gadget-laden sports car and fight evil in a suave and sophisticated way. We will outwardly express this inner world with our walk and talk; we will play Bond music in the car and live in a fantasy world. We have succumbed to the physical and mental influence and absorbed the projected persona of another.

The problem is that James Bond is not real. He is a creation from the mind of not just one man, Ian Fleming, but a great many. For the films are created by producers, directors, writers, and, not least of all, the marketing team. Because we are generally not aware of our true selves we soak up the influences of others, and in time form ourselves into something we are truly not. The work of the alchemist and Gnostic was to eradicate this false influence and discover the real self at the core. It is often equated to peeling an onion—every layer makes us cry, but when we reach the center we find a beautiful, pure white core.

This is the true world of the occult—the world of the hidden—and it is to this hidden world that we must now turn to discover the occult influences upon Ian Fleming.

CHAPTER 6

IAN FLEMING, PART III: OCCULT INFLUENCES

When Ian Fleming finished his schooling, he spent the next few years working as a journalist and formulating around himself varying pockets of friends that he kept in separate groups. In 1939 the Second World War broke out, and Fleming found himself within the world of the secret service, where he would gather more influences and use his knowledge and almost anarchistic brain in the service of his country. Fleming's fascination with the occult, alchemy, and magic would lead him eventually into the arms of the wise old magus (much-hated and much-loved) Aleister Crowley.

It all began in May of 1941, while Fleming was involved in the secretive affairs of military intelligence, when Hitler's deputy, Rudolf Hess, made a stunning parachute jump into Scotland. Hess was a long-term friend of Hitler's. They had been arrested at the Beer Hall Putsch together in 1923, and he had transcribed Hitler's *Mein Kampf*. As far as secret societies and occult belief are concerned, Hess was all the way there as an "intimate" in the Thule Society.

Rudolf Hess was so infamous for his occult fascinations that the whole world seemed to be aware of it, not least because British intelligence would use the fact as propaganda to fool Hess. Although some historians claim that Hess was flying in to bring a new peace treaty, the truth of the matter may be more bizarre. The story goes that Fleming and several other noted intelligence officers, not least of whom was Maxwell, Knight, whom they called "M," devised an outrageous plot to lure Hess to Britain by feeding him false astrological charts. The charts predicted that six planets in the sign of Taurus would coincide with

The Thule Society, or Study Group for Germanic Antiquity, was a German occultist group in Munich named after the mythical northern country from Greek legend. It would later be transformed by Adolf Hitler into the Nazi Party, but had originally been formed in 1918 as a secret society—the Order of the Teutons. They claimed that Ultima Thule was a land founded by Greek and Roman geographers in the furthest north, and that it was the original home of the Aryan race—a theory supported by the widespread ancient discovery of the swastika. These concepts had been fostered previously by theosophists such as Helena Blavatsky, who claimed that this was Plato's Atlantis, and later we find that Aleister Crowley was himself deeply linked with the theosophists.

the full moon, which meant that success would be had for a secret meeting to end the war. Hess had already been fed a false story that certain Scottish elites were going to overthrow Churchill's government, so he decided to fly to Scotland under cover to meet with one of the major plotters—the Duke of Hamilton—who was perfectly aware of the whole ploy.

The whole thing worked perfectly, and Hess, unable to land his plane, simply ditched it and parachuted. For some reason the intelligence services decided not to capitalize on the situation and go public—deciding instead to simply interrogate Hess and then imprison him. It was seemingly sufficient that Hitler's right-hand man had gone missing. In Germany, Hitler set about clamping down on the occult and stating that Hess had simply gone insane—which was rich. As heard on Berlin Radio on May 12:

> A letter which he left behind unfortunately shows by its distractedness traces of mental disorder, and it is feared he was a victim of hallucinations. The Fuhrer at once ordered the arrest of the adjutants of party member Hess, who alone had any cognizance of these flights, and did not, contrary to the Fuhrer's orders, of which they were fully aware, either prevent or report the flight. In these circumstances, it must be considered that party member Hess either jumped out of his plane or has met with an accident.

We do not know whether the whole story of this lure is true or not, as there is little evidence to substantiate it (coming mainly from author and associate of Fleming, Donald McCormick, in *British Secret Service* and

17F: The Life of Ian Fleming). But the KGB did say after the war that the double agent Kim Philby revealed that there had been an SIS plot to lure Hess to Britain via means of forged letters from the Duke of Hamilton.

However, there certainly are hints that astrology was at play in the downfall of Hess, and so the Crowley link later is substantiated—apart from that fact that it is recorded that Crowley was asked to bring his occult knowledge to bear on the matter of Hess's babblings. On the May 14, 1941, the *Volkishcer Beobachter* in Berlin reported: "As is well-known in Party circles, Rudolf Hess was in poor health for many years, and latterly increasingly had recourse to hypnotists, astrologers, and so on. The extent to which these people are responsible for the mental confusion that led him to his present step has still to be clarified."

This indicates that in 1941, the rumors of astrological impropriety were at large. And in 1942 Churchill said to parliament: "When Rudolf Hess flew over here some months ago, he firmly believed that he had only to gain access to certain circles in this country for what he described as 'the Churchill clique' to be thrown out of power and for a government to be set up with which Hitler could negotiate a magnanimous peace."[1]

The whole affair was so politically touchy that the real truth was covered up. Was there a real attempt at signing a peace treaty with Hitler, and was Hess simply a pawn in the game? Was there a British elite, with the likes of the Duke of Hamilton, who were friendly to the Nazi party and therefore willing to overthrow the British government? Or was it all a clever British spy plot? As Churchill wrote in a memorandum: "The Russians are very suspicious of the Hess episode, and I have had a lengthy argument with Marshal Stalin about it at Moscow in October, he stead-fastly maintaining that Hess had been invited over by our Secret Service. It is not in the public interest that the whole of this affair should be stirred at the present moment."[2]

What is fact is that Hess was cap-tured while trying to meet up with someone in Scotland, and he was interrogated. Unfortunately, during the interrogations he spoke in such ridiculous language that nobody could understand him. It seems he had gone completely insane. Be-cause agents knew that Fleming was in contact with and understood the occult, he was called in to help. So Fleming, never one to miss an op-portunity, appealed to one of the most notorious men in British his-tory: Aleister Crowley.

Rudolf Hess

Some researchers claim that, for many years, Fleming had held a keen interest in the legend of the self-titled Great Beast, who was said to be an immensely ugly diabolist and egotistical self-promoter. The fact that Crowley threw himself into the occult without a thought about how the world would consider him seemed to attract Fleming.[3]

Here we come to a distinct understanding in the life of Ian Fleming: that years after his childhood interest in Paracelsus, he was still intrigued in the occult—so much so that he had been fascinated by Crowley.

The interrogators of British Intelligence simply couldn't get any sense out of the ramblings of Hess, so Fleming immediately knew that Crowley would be the man for the job. It was well-known within the world of the secret service that if anybody knew how to get information on the occult, then it would be Ian Fleming. Incredibly, Crowley, who was supposedly living a quiet life writing patriotic war poetry in Torquay, agreed instantly to the project. In his own words: "If it is true that Herr Hess is much influenced by astrology and Magick, my services might be of use to the department in case he should not be willing to do what you wish."[4]

Unfortunately, regardless of popular tradition surrounding Crowley and Fleming, we are told that the actual meeting never occurred, but the account is an indication of Fleming's interest in and knowledge of the subjects of the occult and magic. The very fact that agents within the secret service turned immediately to Ian Fleming is very revealing. They must have known that he himself was interested, and involved with people who were occultists, and I believe that Fleming's links into the occult went much further than is recorded.

Goldeneye

Pierce Brosnan famously starred in the film *Goldeneye*, a James Bond movie that would set the scene for yet more action-packed adventures and reinvigorate the Bond movie scene. But the movie's name was taken from the home of Ian Fleming, and was not a novel.

During the war, Fleming decided to find himself a retreat on the island of Jamaica. His good friend and Jamaican expert, Ivar Bryce, was brought in to find a property. Bryce sent Fleming photographs of a property for sale at £2000 with a hidden beach cove, wilderness, and cliffs, and he fell in love. It was to become his little piece of heaven. We do not know the specific instructions given to Bryce, but we do know that Fleming already knew Jamaica quite well.

Fleming employed a builder and set about making the place barely habitable. For most people, what it was eventually to become was barren and positively stark, but it was exactly what Fleming needed and wanted. He needed a name for it. On occasion he said that the name *Goldeneye* came from a book by Carson McCuller entitled *Reflections in a Golden Eye*, and other times that it was taken from Operation Goldeneye on which he had worked during the war (and had named). However, most likely—and indeed most telling for the alchemical Bond and Fleming—is the fact that the location was called Oracabessa, which is Spanish for "head of gold." In addition, there was indeed a Spanish tomb on the site where was a golden eye set within a golden head.

With the knowledge that Fleming was deeply intrigued and interested in alchemy and the mysteries of the East, it would come as no surprise to discover that he named his "heaven" after something in which he was so engrossed. We know that mystical alchemy came back into Europe following the incursions of Christendom into the Middle East, and I have shown elsewhere that much of this knowledge came back to Europe via the Knights Templar from the mystical elements of Islam—namely the Sufis. Fleming certainly knew of the Templars, for he included a Bill Templar in *Diamonds Are Forever*. The Templars are also well-known to have worshiped the serpent as well as a mysterious head called the Baphomet, and it is my opinion that this is derived from *baphe* (submersion) and *metis* (wisdom), and hence the Templars worshiped the submersion of oneself in wisdom—a distinctly Gnostic and alchemical trait. Idries Shah, the author of *The Sufis*, claims that the Templars' worship of the head was a reference to the transhumanization that takes place within the head of the adherent: "The Golden Head (sar-I-tilai) is a Sufi phrase used to refer to a person whose inner consciousness has been 'transmuted into gold' by means of Sufi study and activity."

Baphomet drawing by Eliphas Levi

This could indeed relate to the Spanish golden head found at Oracabessa, as Sufism in Moorish Spain was not unknown, and it influenced the Spanish mystical world. But did Fleming understand this? From his influences and interests I would suggest that he did. The bookplate image he used for his collection of books has a horned golden goat's head set against a black background—the Fleming clan coat of arms, bearing the motto "Let the

Ian Fleming's bookplate design

Deed Shaw [show]." Baphomet was also imaged as a golden goat's head, and horns are a symbol of enlightenment or illumination.

The "Golden Eye" itself is the vision of the adept—the divine sense and knowledge of the fused or undivided individual. But it is also a term used for the golden proportion—a series of mathematical proportions that, when drawn, form the shape of the eye. These same proportions have been used for thousands of years, and in fact can be seen in the Egyptian Eye of Ra or Eye of Horus. It is a deep esoteric device, revealing understanding of the mysteries of nature. Did Ian Fleming know more than we are led to believe? Did he understand these divine proportions?

Indeed, one of the words that Fleming constantly used was *symmetry*, and it is said that his own drive towards this in his life led him to the point of almost obsessive and compulsive lengths. The cafes and restaurants he ate in and the friends he kept all came under the yoke of his drive for symmetry.[5]

The Golden Eye of God

And I would add that this symmetry extended into the structure he built at Goldeneye (and even its very name)—the place where his muse would flourish. Fleming reveals his understanding of the psychology of symmetry in a series of articles entitled "Thrilling Cities": "...[T]he thwarted or affronted Swiss readily goes, as the psychologists say, 'into paroxysm'.... These states of paroxysm—the reaction of the symmetrist to chaos—are signs of the deep psychosis that results from restraint. They are the lid blowing off the pressure cooker."[6]

According to Fleming, the lack of symmetry creates chaos, and this needed ordering.

One of the images used across the world for the internal balance that Fleming so eagerly sought was the serpent or snake, as we have seen. As I have shown in several books, the snake was used in ancient times across the entire world as a symbol of the internal enlightenment. If Goldeneye was Ian Fleming's soulful retreat, where he needed symmetry and balance, and if Fleming truly understood the ancient alchemical concepts (as depicted by the serpent in all alchemical texts and artwork), then surely the snake would figure in the holy-of-holies that was the Golden Eye.

"But I did get tired of the bedstead and the pictures of snakes he had plastered all over the bedroom wall...."[7] These words of Fleming's infamous friend, Noel Coward, reveal that not only was the snake depicted at Goldeneye, but that they were "plastered all over the bedroom wall." Even the alchemical symbol of the ourobouros—the serpent eating its own tale—would appear in *Live and Let Die* as the Ourobouros Worm and Bait Company, and in *Dr. No*, Bond's girl is believed to have the Voodoo obeah (*ob* means "snake") because she was at peace with snakes wrapped around her neck.

In fact, almost everybody who visited Goldeneye during Fleming's occupation state the same thing about the décor, and that the place was very austere—almost temple-like. It was a place of escape from a world that tipped Fleming out of balance. As he wrote: "If you burden yourself with the big-town malaises you came here to escape—the telephone, gin and canasta jitters, gossip and how to keep up with the procession—those will be the serpents in this Eden."[8]

The Eastern and ancient psychological and esoteric influences upon Fleming were simply part and parcel of the greater mix. As Noel Coward said: "They're very strange people, the Flemings. There's old Peter without a taste bud in his head whizzing through Tibet before the war on a yak and feeding on cow dung. Ian was rather the same at heart."[9]

Of course, one has to wonder how Ian Fleming managed to keep this element of his psyche so secret. The facts are not difficult to discover. Fleming had by the end of the Second World War established himself incredibly deeply within the secret services in Naval intelligence, and it was, quite simply, his job to keep things secret. Following this period, instances of Fleming's esoteric concepts become less and less easy to find. His liking for Paracelsus and Jung almost never figure again until he runs into the mystic Catholic Dame Edith Sitwell.

>●<

What did emerge from his time in the services was his liking for the cell structure. It was and is part of the secret services' (and societies') role to develop cells in all manner of places. Little pockets of individuals would be created and kept separate from each other. Fleming did this with an art that few matched, and he carried it on into his private life. His many and varied friendships were "meticulously insulated" in every area of his life, from the city to the foreign office, in journalism and even in intelligence. Relatively few, if any of his friends seemed to be aware of the process.[10]

He even kept the full extent of his cells from his superiors at the admiralty, which didn't go down well with Admiral Godfrey. It is in this way that Fleming managed to keep his world ordered and symmetrical, and it is also how he managed to keep secret his own inner workings.

Dame Edith Sitwell

One of the later friendships he cherished more than many others was with the poet Dame Edith Sitwell.

Born in Scarborough to the eccentric aristocrat Sir George Sitwell, she claimed descent from the Plantagenets (historical kings of England), and distanced herself from her parents, who she said had been strangers to her. Sitwell's work and interest was deeply mystical—almost Gnostic. By the middle of the 1940s Edith Sitwell was a popular poetess and writer (as were her brothers).

In 1947, Fleming would begin the process of adding Sitwell to his literary and even esoteric cells by inadvertently offending the grand old dame of English poetry. He remarked at a dinner where they were both present that he was amused to find Sitwell's poem "The Shadow of Cain" on the Horizon list (a literary best-of). This in turn infuriated the poet so much that she wrote to Fleming's friend William Plomer about the offense.

In fact, Fleming had never meant to cause offense, and immediately wrote to Sitwell to apologize. The result of this apology was the beginning of a friendship. Sitwell remarked that Fleming's letter could not have been nicer, and he, in his role at the *Times* newspaper, managed to get "The Shadow of Cain" produced in the *Sunday Times*, as a statement of his newfound friendship. At this time Fleming had not yet written a book, but the influence of his new literary cell was growing. He was realizing that these other writers, such as Sitwell, were using their mystical and esoteric leanings within their works, and that he might now do the same.

The influence of Sitwell was profound in more ways than one. Their long conversations led them to discuss the translation Fleming had made of Jung's lecture on Paracelsus, and they even went so far as to discuss publishing the text in book form with endorsements from Sitwell herself. Their shared enthusiasm for the 16th-century alchemist and mystic, and for Jung's interpretation of ancient and sacred secrets, was to foster a lasting love of each other. However, the book never got off the ground.

Casino Royale

When Fleming did finally come around to putting pen to paper with James Bond, he wrote *Casino Royale*, in which he expressed his own mystical experience. His understanding of Jung's concepts of the collective unconscious played out in the writing of the book, which appeared at such a speed from his own unconscious that it amazed him. In this way Fleming was expressing what a great many writers of the esoteric world have expressed: that there was a singular connection between the typewriter and the deeper parts of the human mind. When I myself wrote *Gnosis: The Secret of*

"Certainly with Ian Fleming it was the freedom and depth with which he succeeded in tapping his own unconscious which puts *Casino Royale* in a class by itself among thrillers and adventure stories."[11]

Solomon's Temple Revealed, I experienced the same sense. Before that, I had written books that required huge amounts of research, and were quite frankly a headache to write. When I sat down to write *Gnosis*, however, it all came flooding out of me as though I had opened a gateway to another place, and could no longer hold back the waters.

The truth of the matter, as Jung and many alchemists and mystics have pointed out, is that the knowledge within our own mind, built up throughout years, suddenly hits a point known as the *hundredth monkey principle*, and there is no holding back. This is the principle that when the hundredth monkey is placed into the cage, it can no longer hold them all in, and so bursts, releasing all the monkeys.

When Fleming hit his hundredth monkey, he released a torrent of information within his own mind that had remained in secretive caves for a long time. The wealth of information within Fleming's mind on the secretive world of espionage, and life in general, was to create a wonderful sub-structure for the real Jungian philosophy that was to be revealed in *Casino Royale*.

> "What is so rare about it is that here, encased within the flimsy bodywork of a cheap production-line espionage story, is the essence of this odd man's weird obsession with himself."[12]

And in fact this is the point of gnosis—it is the mystical experience of the Divine within the self, and what is this Divine? It is the point of understanding that releases knowledge and a sense of oneness; it is the key to the hundredth monkey. Fleming laid himself bare in the pages of *Casino Royale* in the same way every writer does, but Fleming had his own issues to play out and his own knowledge of the esoteric and mystical world. He had truly awakened to what he could do. From the opening paragraph of *Casino Royale*: "The scent and smoke and sweat of a casino are nauseating at three in the morning. Then the soul-erosion produced by high gambling—a compost of greed and fear and nervous tension—becomes unbearable, and the senses awake and revolt from it."

In *Casino Royale*, Fleming painted a scene that he was to re-create in varying degrees of success again and again—for within it was the truth he was attempting to state. There was a code within the work that only Jungian philosophers would be able to decipher, as he ably creates both a heroic character and a demonic character. On the one hand we have the knight errant who is on a mission to save the damsel and the world or kingdom, and on the other we have the dark or black knight.

In *Casino Royale* Fleming calls his hero's adversary Le Chiffre, which many believe to be a re-creation of Aleister Crowley—or at least the popular perception of Crowley. This is certainly based upon good reasoning, and is in part true, but there is more: Through the very name he chose he reveals to us what he was doing. *Chiffre* is in fact a French word meaning "cipher" or "code." As Bond says to Le Chiffre: "May I say you are a very important cipher."

Le Chiffre claimed that he was once a Jewish prisoner of Dachau who suffered amnesia, and so could only remember the number on his passport. Fleming is telling us quite blatantly here that there is a code in the book. Now take a look at how this nemesis of Fleming/Bond dies in the actual book when shot: "...[A]nd suddenly Le Chiffre had grown another eye, a third eye on a level with the other two, right where the thick nose started to jut out below the forehead. It was a small black eye, with no eyelashes or eyebrows."

By working through the cipher, or code, the ultimate realization would be attained, and the third eye opened. It is code upon code, beautifully written. In *Casino Royale*, Fleming has Le Chiffre serving a "wonderful purpose" and a really "vital purpose," which he states to be the highest purpose of all, that his existence as the evil counterpart was actually creating a norm of badness by which alone an opposing goodness could exist. By destroying Le Chiffre, Bond had somehow destroyed himself, or at least the reason for his own existence. However, Bond claims that he had been privileged to have been able to "see" the evil nature for what it truly was, and that he has emerged a better and more virtuous man.

Le Chiffre became the ultimate hook upon which to hang the various coats of his future villains—many of whom would also have ciphered names. The fact that Fleming kept this deeper understanding of the forces of human nature (and indeed the very universe) to himself, or at least within a very select few, explains why other biographers have only vaguely crossed this path—for it is seemingly impossible to prove. And yet as one builds up the picture of Ian Fleming and his contacts and interests in the world of the esoteric, one finds that there is more to the man. The very fact that Fleming claimed to have spawned *Casino Royale* from his unconsciousness and that it was "an experiment in the autobiography of dreams"[13] reveals quite a lot. Fleming knew that his was a divided mind, that he had striven his entire life to meet the false ideals he created with the aid of a dominating mother (M) and an almost-too-perfect brother. Bond was now his method of placing these thoughts, dreams, desires, and nightmares on paper, and correcting them in the Jungian fashion.

"[A]bove all he liked it that everything was one's own fault. There was only oneself to praise or blame."[14] Ian Fleming was himself also at fault, for the dualities in his life, and he knew it. To accept responsibility for one's own actions and thoughts was and always shall be the first step upon the ladder to higher things. But this recognition seemed to cut at his love of symmetry, and bring chaos. He laid out this chaos within the natures of his villains. It is said that he always had trouble with his villains, as he may also have had with his heroines, and the reason is simple: his obsession with symmetry, the balance within the book. In each new novel he gave new faces to the same old underlying base, a new mask for his ideal "Crowley."[15]

These villains were the repressed parts of himself—of the dark side that we all have. They were the demonic aspects of ourselves, termed *chaos* by many or *shadow* by Jung, but all too often allowed to roam free in this world. Fleming loads his villains with his own internal and external struggle. The negative elements of his own mind and the form are placed upon the bad guy, as if bearing his own soul and yet also hiding. He sends in his alter-ego hero James Bond to do battle with his dark nature, the light to overcome the dark.

At Fleming's funeral, his close friend William Plomer, who had known him probably closer than most, said that it was possible for James Bond and his adventures to become infamous because of their realism and detail, but also because of the ancient romantic fairy-tale myths that underlay them. He said that they fulfilled a constant need within mankind, the age-old need to escape from the dullness by seeing oneself as the dragon-slaying hero, battling the devilish forces of darkness that lay within our very selves. By taking on these self-born dark natures we became stronger people.

How true the words of one of Fleming's closest friends—that Fleming was re-creating those same old fairy tales to fulfil our inner desires. What we are finding in our search through the life of this peculiar writer is exactly what Plomer then went on to say "that the popular image of him is far too crude and flat."[16] If anybody should know the truth of this complex writer, it should be his closest friend.

We are all divided, and only by uniting the two elements of our mind can we overcome the chaos of madness that is the adversary of James Bond. As a literary alchemist Ian Fleming knew that he must have the tools of the trade, and as any alchemist attempted to turn base metal into gold, Ian Fleming turned his ordinary base metal typewriter in for a golden one. And he wished to keep his reasoning secret: "I will not tell you why I am acquiring this machine...."[17]

In fact, Fleming even suggested to playwright Enid Bagnold (author of *National Velvet*) that she should write a play about hidden gold, in which the treasure was not real gold at all. In a letter to Bagnold he claimed that a psychoanalyst once explained to him at length that treasure-hunting was the perfect example of the weakness of character that makes the individual search for shortcuts to happiness, and that it distracted from the reality of living. The *true* search for *real* gold would enable the individual to "cock a snook" at authority, and have everything your own way.[18]

As for Enid Bagnold herself, she does have certain links within the esoteric cell of Ian Fleming (apart from the fact that she was addicted to morphine—a drug that opens the mind to altered states—for 60 years). She was seduced upstairs in the Café Royal (sounds like a Bond novel to me) by a certain Frank Harris, a publisher, author, and journalist who lived for some time with Aleister Crowley. The links in this occult circle are there, and yet left out of standard biographies. For instance, most of this elite literary cell were involved in what was called the Bloomsbury Set, and one only needs to dig a little to discover that addresses given by such orders as the Ordo Templi Orientis, a magical, modern Knights Templar organization overseen for a long period by Aleister Crowley himself, matched those of the Bloomsbury Set.

Both Fleming and his publisher and friend, William Plomer, were involved with this erudite bunch, which began in the previous century as a kind of socialist elite, but was often related to secret societies and arcane goings-on, including those of the secret society known as the Cambridge Apostles. Members of this group were called *apostles* because it began with 12 members, and they have been accused of many things, not least of which is the fact that angels or ex-members have gone on to become powerful people in positions of great authority. The group came to public attention in 1951 with the exposure of the Cambridge Spy Ring, where two former members were found to be working for the KGB within the British government. Indeed, the infamous Guy Burgess (MI6/KGB) and Anthony Blunt (MI5/KGB) were both Cambridge Apostles. A friend and intelligence colleague of Fleming's, Donald McCormick (alias Richard Deacon), actually wrote a book about them.

In the *Morning Post* on January 19, 1931, the Bloomsbury Black Mass was exposed to the world, as well as links across the country to other "Black Mass" gatherings. Due to various misunderstandings mixed with a great deal of truth, these Black Mass gatherings were quite opposite from the collective Christian England we find in black-and-white propaganda films of the period.

The Rosicrucian Order

Another one of these secretive orders that Fleming would often come across was the Rosicrucian Order, and many historians are now pointing towards Dr. John Dee as playing a major role in laying the foundations of this movement, quite apart from Fleming's own mother's maiden name being St. Croix-Rose, and Fleming himself having come into contact with many Rosicrucians via the Bloomsbury Set. Indeed, many have "fixed the origin of this sect at the...theories of Paracelsus and the dreams of Dr. Dee, who without intending it, became the actual, though never recognised founders of the Rosicrucian philosophy."[19]

The Rosicrucian Order has many legends, and not so much fact. The earliest recorded documentation is from the 17th century (although earlier organizations must have existed), and people such as Cornelius Agrippa (who was employed by Henry VIII for a time), Dr. John Dee, Paracelsus, and Francis Bacon are cited as instigators of its creation. This would make complete sense, because not only were Dee and Bacon involved in the world of the esoteric (and, therefore, secrecy), but also the world of the secret service. In Fleming's time the Nazis would accuse the British secret service of still being very much under the influence of the Rosicrucian Brotherhood. The Rosicrucian "coincidences" surrounding Ian Fleming seem to be veering toward some form of membership—or at the very least, deeper knowledge of the group—and these coincidences will grow as we move forward.

Rosy Cross or Rosicrucian

In the early 1600s there were formed a brotherhood of seven, called collectively the Rose-Croix. The number was used for esoteric reasons (just as Fleming would use it for Bond). Their goal was to bring spiritual enlightenment to humankind—to reveal the inner world and the "chemical wedding" of Christian Rosenkreuz, named after the fabled founder—the Christian rose and cross. Legend states that this fabled pilgrim spent time with various masters in the Middle East and then returned to Europe to bring his enlightenment, which appeared in three manifestoes in the 17th century. There are mystical Islamic connections to it, and it is believed that Sufi concepts as well as Gnostic thought are intertwined, as they always are, within the manifestoes, in the golden head or golden eye.

> The oral history passed down is that the movement actually was a continuation of a broad, ancient esoteric tradition that only included Hermetic gnosticism. Hermetic gnosticism had been built upon by Magi throughout the previous centuries, and was constantly protected from loss or destruction through the various arcane methods, partly through word of mouth from a lineage of leaders selected initiatically by each generation to carry on the sacred tradition.[20]

As the Rosicrucians claimed in *Rosae Rubeae et Aureae Crucis*:

> Know that the Order of the Rose and Cross has existed from time immemorial, and that its mystic rites were practiced and its wisdom taught in Egypt, Eleusis, Samothrace, Persia, Chaldea, India, and in far more ancient lands, and thus handed down to posterity the Secret Wisdom of the Ancient Ages. Many were its Temples, and among many nations were they established, though in process of time some lost the purity of their primal knowledge.

They designated themselves as "invisibles," and their fabled founder, Christian Rosenkreuz, is said to have written the handbook on magic entitled simply *M*, for *Magicon*. This magic very much revolved around magnetism and balance—a subject on which Ian Fleming would collect a great many books. Gustav Bord wrote, in *La Franc-Macionnerie en France*, in 1908, with reference to this hidden subject of the Rosicrucians and the knowledge of Paracelsus: "The doctrine of Paracelsus was drawn from the Cabala, Hermetic philosophy, and alchemy. He claimed to know and expound the entire system of the Mysterious forces which act in nature and in man.... Man must unite himself to the forces required in order to produce either physical or intellectual phenomena. The Universe was the Macrocosm, man was the Microcosm, and they were similar...."

It seems peculiar to the outside world that secret services and intelligence agencies should be so tied in to the world of secret orders and magic, but the fact remains a constant one. Gustav Bord tells us later in his book: "In all times there were secret sects who claimed to understand the laws which regulate the Universe; some believed they really possessed the ineffable secret; others, the clever ones, made their mysteries a lure for the crowd; claiming thus to dominate and lead it; at least they found the way to utilize it to their profit."

Dr. John Dee was a foundation for the Rosicrucian movement, an expert alchemist, mathematician, astrologer, collector of fine books, and spy for the state. Fleming would learn of Dee and of the world of the esoteric and continue the Hermetic teachings in his novels. Through his own separated cells Fleming had contacts in a great many worlds, he saw the Gnostic truth behind these various organizations and understood their ideas. When we understand that the reason behind the formation of secret societies is very often in the realm of higher human thought, and that the members then believe that the rest of humankind ought to have this knowledge, there is little wonder that these men find their way into positions of power in order to set about the change. The Rosicrucians have always been one of those groups, claiming to have hermetic or esoteric knowledge, so for the good of humankind they must therefore infiltrate the power base. It worked in the time of Dee, it worked a century or so later with Adam Weishaupt and the infamous Illuminati, and it seemed to have worked again in the time of Ian Fleming with the Bloomsbury Set and other groups, all influenced by the dawning of a new age of enlightened thought and secret societies.

In a pamphlet from the 1930s by Dr. Wynn Westcott, the Supreme Magus of Societas Rosicruciana in Anglia, published by Watkins in London, we have the following statement:

> The revived Rosicrucian Lodges on the Continent of Europe are carried on with great privacy, and their members do not openly confess to their admission and membership. Several centers are in active work under conditions derived from previous centuries of usefulness...they also teach and practice curative effects of colored light, and cultivate mental processes which are believed to induce spiritual enlightenment and extended powers of the human senses.

Within these groups there was always a Master, denoted as M. In *The Masters* by Annie Besant (1912), we read:

> A Master is a term applied by Theosophists to denote certain human beings, who have completed their human

evolution, have attained human perfection.... Those who are named M. (Morya)...were Masters who founded the Theosophical Society, using Colonel Olcott and H.P. Blavatsky, both disciples of M., to lay its foundations.... Blavastky...met M. on the bank of the Serpentine, when she visited London in 1851.

One has to wonder just why M figures so prominently as the Master of our man of light, James Bond. And we also have to ask whether Fleming based his secretive groups for world domination, namely SMERSH and SPECTRE, upon groups such as the Golden Dawn, Rosicrucians, and Freemasons. Max Heindel, the occultist, mystic, and astrologer, said in his 1911 book, the *Rosicrucian Cosmo-Conception*: "Thus, all over the world the old systems of paternal government are changing. Nations as such have had their day, and are unwittingly working towards Universal brotherhood in accordance with the design of our invisible leaders, who are nonetheless potent in shaping events because they are not officially seated in the councils of nations."

British intelligence logo for M15

The Rosicrucians even claimed to have taken part in international political conventions. From the growing links within the world of Fleming and his own knowledge and methods of secrecy, I was rapidly gaining the notion that he was involved in much more than just the secret service. Indeed, even MI5 has a logo, which contains the pyramid and the all-seeing eye.

►◄

One of the people Fleming knew from within the world of the esoteric, and from whom he gathered much knowledge, was Geoffrey Watkins, who later started a publishing company. According to the publisher's Website, which gives a short history of the publishing company (that I myself was published by twice):

> As a child Geoffrey met many of the leading occult figures of the time; MacGregor Mathers, W.B. Yeats, George Russell, Aleister Crowley, all visited the shop, and A.E. Waite was a lifelong friend of Geoffrey Watkins, as were many other occult authors. His schooldays were spent in Heidelberg, and when he returned to England he was fluent in German. He planned to become a lawyer but the turmoil in Europe that resulted in the Great War thrust him into service. He was commissioned into Bristish Military Intelligence in 1914 and was "kept busy in that field" until 1919. He may have even aided the wily Crowley on his hilarious anti-German propaganda commissions from the Royal Navy Admiralty, just down the road.

The gathering storm-heads of a new war had taken a far darker turn by the late Thirties, and Geoffrey was drawn quickly back into the shadow-world of Intelligence fieldwork again in 1939.

I spoke to one of the publishers at Watkins, who informed me that Geoffrey had in fact been involved in producing astrological charts for Churchill, and in all likelihood helping Ian Fleming in the deceit that they were to plot for Rudolf Hess. Ian Fleming, it seems, was much more than an ordinary writer; he was involved with some of Britain's best and brightest in the occult worlds, who were influencing government at the very highest levels in both Britain and Germany.

Another one of Fleming's acquaintances was Sefton Delmer, a journalist Fleming met while on an undercover mission to spy on the Russians in 1939. They became friends, and soon Delmer's knowledge of the occult would become handy as he helped set up a radio station for "black propaganda." "Of the more bizarre intentions, on March 9th, 1942, Delmer announced that he wanted an 'Occult' station, G6, to start by the end of the week.... As for the total results of the black broadcasters, only under the direction of Sefton Delmer did the whole endeavor become really effective, operating from the purpose-built transmission center at Milton Bryan, from 1943."[21]

It was in fact Ian Fleming who requested of Naval intelligence that Sefton Delmer be the man behind this powerful propaganda tool. Delmer had an extraordinary ability to empathize with the German mind, having been born in Berlin to an Austrian father, and was a professor in English at Berlin University. By 1917 the family had been repatriated into England, Delmer achieved a degree at Oxford, and then returned to Berlin as correspondent for the *Daily Express*. During his time there, Delmer actually became personally acquainted with the top members of the Nazi elite, including Hitler, Goebbels, Himmler, and Hess.

By 1940, Delmer had realized that he needed to do something to help the English cause, but at 17 stone he was simply too out of shape for active combat. He approached Ian Fleming, whom he knew to be linked with Naval intelligence. At first, the recruiters were wary of this repatriated ex-German and Nazi associate, and considered him to be a prime candidate to be a Nazi double-agent. Eventually, however, he got clearance, and was soon placed in charge of a clandestine radio station broadcasting to Germany as if it were a German station.

Very quickly, Naval intelligence (but more specifically, Ian Fleming) saw the potential of black propaganda, and soon, with the aid of Delmer, crafted it into a sleek and powerful machine—which they could only have done with occult knowledge and contacts. By 1942, Delmer was using the occult as a tool directly aimed at the elite of the Nazi party that he knew so well. At the same time, Ian Fleming was maintaining contacts within the world of the occult, such as Dennis Wheatley (who worked for the London Controlling Section, masterminding deception projects) and Louis de Wohl (who was used as an astrologer by Naval intelligence to chart Hitler's movements and give Naval Intelligence advanced warning).

Ludwig Von Wohl-Musciny, or Louis de Wohl, was a Hungarian astrologer who headed the "black group," the British group of astrologers used by the Department of Psychological Warfare linked intricately to Fleming's office. De Wohl was chosen for the role because of his knowledge of the techniques of Karl Ersnt Krafft, the Nazi astrologer.

His job, and that of his underlings, was to use astrology to anticipate what the German elite were being advised by their astrologers. However, it turned out that de Wohl had somewhat overstated his talents, and the Secret Service soon rumbled him, and he was sacked. He did, however, help with the war effort, and produced anti-Nazi propaganda based upon astrological predictions and the work of the 16th-century seer, Nostradamus.

As we discover more and more connections in the world of the occult, we find that Fleming's cell was really quite broad. All the elements of the occult are discovered in the influences upon Fleming, from alchemy to gnostic thought, from astrology to numerology, because all were part and parcel of the same "hidden knowledge." We are also finding some broken links—the rough and jagged edges of once-connected strands of history. Somewhere the strands were snapped, and I believe that although a lot of the blame can be laid at the door of the secret services for the security of the realm, there is equal blame upon Fleming, for hiding his own role. This was a common theme in the life of Ian Fleming, and something all biographers discover—that he kept parts of his life not just at a distance from one another, but often totally secret, or eradicated them altogether.

CHAPTER 7

RELIGION, PHILOSOPHY, AND TELEVISION

Ian Fleming described his stories as "fairy tales for grown-ups."[1] The question is, was Fleming implying here his knowledge of the fact that traditional fairy tales held a deeper wisdom for us? Fairy tales are exactly that: tales of fairies, and these were the wise ones of old who went to ground to escape the sins of the modern age.

In both orthodox biographies of Ian Fleming, by Andrew Lycett and John Pearson, almost nothing is said about Fleming's religious or spiritual beliefs. There are instances that reveal him to be close to Catholicism (or at least the mystical element implied), but nothing is said of a belief. As James Bond was modeled on a side of Ian Fleming he wished to more fully be, then we ought to find Fleming's beliefs hidden within the character. Luckily, we don't have to dig, because Fleming himself pointed it out. He said that the world of Bond was a Manichean one.

Now some have taken this to mean that Bond's world mirrored that of the geopolitical world of the time, with East against West, and this may be true. But with the knowledge that Ian Fleming meant much more when he spoke about Bond being Manichean, we must delve deeper.

Mani

The name *Mani* derives from the Persian prophet Mani (AD 210–276). Although few of his writings are still in existence, his legacy continues. In fact, the name isn't real; it is instead a title assumed by the founder. Many scholars believe that St. Augustine carried on the Manichean thoughts into Christianity, as he himself was a convert from the Manichean faith. From the Persian province of Babylon in the third century this new way spread far and wide, reaching as far as China and North Africa. Through-out the course of 10 centuries the original angels or deities adapted and changed according to location, but the one source center, or the Father of Light, remained virtually the same, as the "original man."

The call to humankind was to step from darkness into the light of the original man, and so it was dualistic. In fact, now we can see clearly what Fleming meant when he called James Bond Manichean, for Bond is in-deed the man of light stepping out of the darkness of Fleming himself, imaged on paper as the villain.

Mani claimed to have received a revelation as a child from a spirit guide he called "the twin." This spirit taught him divine truths, which he wrote down and taught to others. This twin or true self enabled Mani to self-realize. This is known as *gnosticus* or *gnosis*—the knowledge of divine truths. And so the Manichean faith, as spoken of by Ian Fleming, is gnosis. It is the mystical experience of the Divine in the Self, and this true

Self is the original man of light. If Fleming is telling us that James Bond is Manichean, then is he depicting him as a Gnostic man of light? Bond is in fact Fleming's literary twin.

> Mani's disciples spread to Palestine, Greece, Italy, Gaul, Scythia, the Danube, and Africa. His doctrine was for centuries propagated by oral tradition, often under different names...such as the Cathars, Albigenses, the Templars, and the Brothers of St. John of Jerusalem. In the fifteenth century esoteric Christianity, inspired by the same tradition, became more laic and scientific under the influence of the Cabala and alchemy, and it was about then that Christian Rosenkreutz founded the Order of the Rose-Croix.[2]

It seems James Bond could trace his heritage back a very long way—the question is, does his name also reveal any of this Manichean influence that Fleming claimed?

The Name—James Bond

The biblical James is the brother of Jesus, and has been equated with Thomas (Didymus, meaning "twin"), but the etymology of James reveals that it is another form of Jacob, which means "supplanter." So this twin supplants another, and that other is Ian Fleming. In this way, James is a literary twin supplanting the real Ian Fleming.

Jacob, in the Bible, was born grasping at the heel of his brother Esau and later bought his birthright. There is a subtlety to this name that is only revealed when we understand Fleming's Manichean (twin spirit revelation) and gnostic concepts. Fleming must have laughed at the ingenuity of this etymology, for he too was born virtually grasping at his elder brother's heels. There is absolutely no reason for Fleming to have revealed this ingenious use of names, and in his usual fashion he would give "ordinary" and "plain" reasons for the use of "boring" names. If nothing else, Ian Fleming was good at mocking his public.

18th-century depiction of Joachim and Boaz

The surname, Bond, on the other hand, means "to bind." It is a form of covenant or testament, and James Bond is the new testament or man of light—the Manichean savior. There is almost a subtle jealousy in the meaning of the words—a kind of twin on paper that Ian Fleming wished to be. Manicheanism was an uncompromising system of dualism; a conflict between light and darkness, good and evil. Darkness sought to bind men, light to set them free—light was the ultimate savior, the good brother.

Boaz and Joachim

But the twin is also revealed in the initials themselves, so often seen on briefcases, guns, and all manner of Bond gadgets. In Freemasonry the twin pillars of Joachim and Boaz, or J and B, are and have been depicted across the world for hundreds of years in lodges and sacred artworks and texts. These pillars represent the twin concepts of balance, and we must walk between the pillars in the neutral and perfectly balanced state if we are to reach the holy of holies in the temple within—wherein lies our true self. With his links into Freemasonic knowledge, Fleming must have known of this clever device.

John Calvin

Fleming also said that James Bond was educated at a Calvinist school. This Protestant sect, named after the founder, John Calvin, taught that humanity was fallen, and morally and spiritually unable to follow God or even escape their own condemnation unless God decided so. In this way there is nothing anybody can do to get into heaven; it is all God's will. The individual must believe in the gospel and admit his or her faith before God can decide, but that by no means guarantees the keys to the Pearly Gates. Fleming's understanding of the Calvinist way is clear, and it is obvious why he chose this background for James Bond, as it allowed him the scope to be amoral and yet dedicated to the duty of saving the world. Similar to the Calvinist doctrine, Bond is a slave to the duty he is given, and hates sloth and laziness. The death of his opponents is almost not an issue, because God himself has already chosen, by Calvinist predestination, who shall enter heaven. Bond was in essence God's man of light on earth—here to dish out death and set this darkness into order.

The Serpent

According to true Gnostic form we should have a serpent or dragon involved in the tale in a great many ways, and we should have a union or infusion of serpent wisdom within the character of Bond. The early Gnostics themselves were often termed the *ophites*, or serpent-worshipers, and held that Christ was the good serpent. Bond is the dragon-slayer, the one who controls the power of the dark nature. The serpent and dragon imagery from our religious and mythical past is both good and bad, positive and negative. Overcoming the powerful serpent or dragon was to crush the fiery aspect of our nature with truth and wisdom—the elements of the Sophia. Bond's infamous nemesis Dr. No was equated with the serpent by the spy himself: "The bizarre, gliding figure looked like a giant venomous worm wrapped in grey tin-foil, and Bond would not have been surprised to see the rest of it trailing slimily along the carpet behind."[3]

Of course, a worm is a small, wriggling insect and not a snake, but the origin and etymology of the word shows that it actually derives from *orm* for "serpent," and was in fact seen as a small snake. Dr. No was hardly being equated with a small worm, but a large serpent, gliding. Bond was to overcome this dark nature, the negative serpent or dragon, as all good dragon slayers—defeating the dark nature and uniting once again with his feminine principle, the Bond girl. This was the sacred marriage, and what is little known is that James Bond did actually marry.

Her name was Teresa (Tracy) di Vincenzo. The etymology of her name is revealing: As Bond was the Manichean man of light, so *Teresa* actually means "summer." And Vincenzo was the name of a famous alchemist, Vincenzo Cascariolo, of Bologna, Italy, whose passion it was to discover the Philosopher's Stone. Instead, Cascariolo discovered Barium sulphate, known as lapis solaris—the sun stone.

Teresa was the daughter of Marc-Ange Draco, and an English governess. Due to her marriage with Count Guido di Vincenzo, her surname was cleverly hidden. She had a child with the count who died following her divorce, and she became self-destructive. She was rescued by Bond and they married—uniting the two lights—but the Bond nemesis Blofeld shot Teresa and killed her. Bond gets his revenge and evens up the Manichean imbalance by killing Irma Bunt, Blofeld's lover, and then Blofeld himself.

James Bond's mother was killed in a climbing accident in the Aiguilles Rouges of Switzerland. Her name was Monique Delacroix. Taking the name apart we have Monique, which is the French version of Monica and is derived from the Italian word *monacco* for "monk" (solitary), which is itself derived from the Greek *mono*. So she is a very singular lady. Her surname indeed gives us several insights: In 1927, the year Fleming gave up Eton as a lost cause, a study on the use of psychotropic drugs was begun by Walter Benjamin (1892–1940) entitled *Protocols to the Experiments on Hashish, Opium and Mescaline.*[4] In this unique study Benjamin explains the effects of his second hashish experience in 1928:

> The recollection is less vivid although the reverie was of a diminished intensity compared to the first time. To be precise, I was not as lost in thought, but more profoundly inward. Also, the gloomy, strange, exotic passage of the rausch haunt the recollection more than the luminous ones.
>
> I recall a satanic phase. The red of the walls became the determining factor for me. My smile took on satanic features: although it assumed more the expression of satanic knowledge, satanic satisfaction, satanic repose than the satanic, destructive effect. The sense of those present in the room as being submerged intensified: the room became more velvety, more glowing, darker. I named it Delacroix.

Ian Fleming knew of Benjamin's work, and Benjamin certainly wrote about Fleming's. In fact, both were speaking of and creating icons for society. Could Fleming have taken one of Benjamin's icons—his dark, drug-induced, otherworldly experience—and forged it into his monkish mother? Was this his real mother coming through in Bond's? A subtle way of expressing his inner thoughts about his own controlling maternal guide? As Andrew Lycett said in his biography of Ian Fleming, she was quite often a little more than "overbearing."

Of course, Fleming was infamous for using etymology or word play in his characters' names, and here, in Monique Delacroix, we have the "monk of the cross," the one who wishes to be "alone with the cross." She died at the hand of the red ridges of Aiguilles Rouge (hand-needle, red, red-hot).

Collections

Ian Fleming collected books and articles for personal interests and research. Many of these are now in the Lilly Library at Indiana University. Taking a look at this collection gives us an insight into the mind of Fleming, and his deeper interests.

He certainly seemed to have a deep interest in agnosticism and the religious responses, as he collected "Agnosticism" by T.H. Huxley (excerpt from *The Nineteenth Century*, vol. 25, no. 144, pp. 169–194, February, 1889), and all the various responses to this article by theologians and experts. This is not a surprise, as Fleming grappled with his own religious beliefs.

Another interestingly philosophical and possitively alchemical article was "Theory of the earth; or an investigation of the laws observable in the composition, dissolution, and restoration of land upon the globe," by James Hutton, (article no. 10, excerpt from *Philosophical Transactions*, 209–304, read March 7, and April 4, 1785, journal dated 1785), as well as "On a new fulminating mercury," by Edward Howard, Esq., (article no. 11, excerpt from *Philosophical Transactions*, 204–238, read March 13, 1800, periodical dated 1800). In fact, Fleming's collection of chemical articles reads very much as if he were trying to discover the secret of transforming lead into gold. They also relate heavily to the modern work of the Rosicrucians, which dealt with the world of modern chemistry and alchemy.

Several books in his collection are of interest. One of them was *Principes du droit politique* by Jean-Jacques Rousseau (Amsterdam, 1762). The text from the Lilly Library catalogue describes this entry from Rousseau (1712–1778) as being fundamentally at odds with the beliefs of the establishment: "In the Age of Reason he advocated the greater force of intuition: against artificial refinement, he urged a return to the natural state. So, defying the absolute monarchy of France, he published his exposition of the social contract, never more clearly or powerfully stated, that government is dependent upon the mandate of the people. It had a profound influence on French political thought, and was perhaps more directly the cause of the Revolution than any other single factor."

Another interesting title was *Essai sur L'Inégalité des Races Humaines* by Joseph-Arthur Comte de Gobineau (Paris, 1853–1855). It was Gobineau who said that race was permanent and unchangeable, proclaiming that the Aryan or Nordic race was the elite, and should rule the world. The Nazis took this and used it to their own ends. It is interesting to see Fleming owning such a text, considering his Germanic tendencies from his early days, and the Golden Dawn and Rosicrucian links speak volumes.

Fleming had several books on the psychological front, among them Sigmund Freud's *Die Traumdeutung* (Leipzig and Vienna, 1900), which was Freud's greatest work of psychoanalytical concepts, the erotic nature of dreams, and the theory of the unconscious self. Another interesting addition considering Fleming's understanding of unconsciousness and sleep was *Neurypnology, or the Rationale of Nervous Sleep, Considered in Relation With Animal Magnetism. Illustrated by Numerous Cases of its Successful Application in the Cure of Disease* by James Braid (London, 1843). The Lilly Library comments that the author introduced the term *hypnotism* and demonstrated that it could be self-induced by fixing one's gaze upon inanimate objects. The mental concentration proved that the subjective or personal nature of the act was key, and not necessarily external influences such as mesmerism. This, it is said, led to violent opposition from devotees of Mesmer, among them Edgar Allan Poe, who profoundly influenced Fleming.

Interestingly, the library has Ian Fleming's own copy of *Casino Royale*, with an inscription on the fly leaf in Fleming's hand, outlining his own turmoil with regard to marriage and affection: "This was written in January and February, 1952, accepted by Cape [the publisher] in the Spring and published a year later."

Fleming points out that the book was written as a focus to take his mind off other matters at Goldeneye, and that the characters were not based on real people. These "other matters at Goldeneye" he claims were his marriage: "Marriage, a chilling description; but revealing of the author's capacity for affection, love and human relations. I F, June 12th, 1963."

It is interesting to note, that although Fleming often claimed his characters were based upon real people, here he yet again contradicts himself and says that they were not. He is also apparently surprised at his own capacity for love and "human relations."

The Prisoner

In the 1950s and '60s spy novels and films erupted into the popular culture, and there they remained for decades. Some have attributed this to the Cold War, but whatever the reason, it was good timing for Ian Fleming, as suddenly the now incredibly popular Bond novels were sought out by the film studios. As these and other spy films became hits overnight television producers jumped on the bandwagon and started making spy shows. One of the most popular was *Dangerman/Secret Agent* staring Patrick McGoohan as John Drake (dragon). However, as this series came to an end, McGoohan and George Markstein decided to create a new series. Called *The Prisoner*, the series features the strange life of a top-secret agent (played by McGoohan) who resigns his post for reasons that are never revealed. He then drives home and starts packing his suitcase. His home is gassed and he awakens in what appears to be the same place hours later. In fact, this new home is a recreation of his flat in London, and outside he finds a peculiar village full of similar prisoners. This is an otherworldly experience, accessed in dream. It is in fact taking Dangerman/McGoohan into himself to purge him of all that is wrong in his life. It is a distinctly alchemical process, and one that Bond himself goes through in each book, and indeed to some extent, film. Reduction and re-creation is the constant drive of the alchemist.

We are never told the Prisoner's name; just his number: 6. All the other "residents" have numbers too, with the boss, who changes every episode, being Number 2. We never actually see who Number 1 is. Throughout the whole short series each Number 2 attempts to find out some secret and hidden knowledge from within McGoohan's mind, and all fail. Number 6 makes it his role to thwart their attempts, and escape. It is a fantastic piece of psychological battling, and has drawn the attention of hundreds of different viewpoints. In the end Number 6 escapes with each character of Number 2, which are elements of himself he cannot leave behind. He is in fact battling with himself the whole way through the series. We can see this in the opening statement of each show: Number 6 asks Number 2, "Who is Number 1?" to which Number 2 responds, "You are, Number 6."

The author in Portmeirion

McGoohan, who produced the show, wrote much of the content, and even directed many of the episodes under various pseudonyms, has religiously refused to explain the exact meanings behind the various elements of the show. However, there are similarities between *The Prisoner* and the James Bond books that reveal that McGoohan and others were spoofing Bond. In fact, at the end of the *Dangerman* series McGoohan was asked to play Bond by the producers, but he refused, saying only that he could not associate with one of the people on the team. It is difficult to say who this person was, as several actors are to be found on both sides of the camp in both *The Prisoner* and the Bond films. The *Prisoner* episode "The Girl Who Was Death," contains many similarities to the Bond films: A shoeshine has a phone built in to his kit, and the wisecracks are very Bondian. There are dozens of similarities in many of the episodes, and McGoohan has never denied the claim that Number 6 was a parody of Bond, not least because *Dangerman* itself was a copy of Bond, and even featured a Q character issuing gadgets.

There are many social and psychological statements in the series, playing on the needs of the individual as opposed to those of the state in which he lives. In an interview in 1982, Patrick McGoohan said: "It was about the most evil human being, human essence, and that is ourselves. It is within each of us. That is the most dangerous thing on the Earth, what is within us. So, therefore, that is what I made Number 1—oneself—an image of oneself which he was trying to beat."[5]

McGoohan is pointing out here that the dark nature of man needs to be overcome—that it is extremely dangerous, as history has shown. This darkness is the shadow side of our selves that needs to be constantly battled. Symbolically, McGoohan only wanted the series to be seven episodes long, but compromised with the TV studio, which wanted 26. The battle that McGoohan was portraying was age-old—the fight for the individual, and freedom against the oppression of humankind. Constantly we are told that reality as we know it may not be precisely true, and that it is in fact a series of constructs from society at large formulated from within the mind of man. Number 6 fights this mind-bending series of reality trials again and again in order to discover himself and maintain his freedom of mind and spirit, even though his body may be trapped. It is a good lesson to us all, for society, created by man, would have us all in psychological chains if we allowed it. From the debt and credit cycles that keep us running blindly on the hamster-wheel of work, to the religious and socio-political deceit with which we are continually bombarded. Be good, we are told, and then screw everybody else to get what we want. Maintaining a sense of balance and self-awareness in this barrage of mental abuse is what *The Prisoner* represents.

In essence, as does James Bond, *The Prisoner* plays out an ancient fairy tale in a modern format. This is the real reason for the longevity of stories such as those surrounding the Holy Grail, Robin and Marion, James Bond, and Number 6—they represent something we all recognize, whether consciously or subconsciously. The village in which Number 6 was trapped was the fanciful world we all live in—as real as anything we believe. In the episode "The Chimes of Big Ben," Number 6 escapes and makes it back to London, where he asks: "I risked my life...to come back here, home, because I thought it was different... It is, isn't it? Isn't it different?"

In truth, wherever we are, we take our mind, and it is within the mind that we struggle—the world around us, as McGoohan himself said, is a myth. The elusive Number 1 was in fact Number 6—he was Oneness, he fought against himself. And of course, 1 and 6 makes 7. And even Number 6's car was a Lotus Seven*, with the number plate KAR 120C, the meaning of which nobody knows (*kar* in etymology means "hard," and 120C could be 120 cubits, for the height of the Temple of Jerusalem—the symbol of the perfect man*).

According to John W. Whitegead, the saving grace of *The Prisoner*, and its importance, was in Patrick McGoohan's belief in the dignity and worth of humankind:

> That tiny spark of divinity that has been inlaid in our conscience enables us from time to time to recognize the superficiality of the world around us. It is true that we are all numbered. We are surrounded by police, neighbours who watch and inform on us, cameras and a pervasive technology, but we can will ourselves to fight the stranglehold of conformity and express our individuality. And even though we are all prisoners, we can raise our fists against oppression and scream, "I am not a number, I am a free man!"[6]

The Prisoner as a creation has its own symbolic codes, just as do the James Bond novels. The Penny Farthing bicycle seen in each show as a logo device for the Village represented continuation of progress, as stated by McGoohan. The umbrella motif that was neither black nor white represented the neutral state we need to be in to overcome the imbalance of the positive and negative states of mind.

Although the time frames mean that *The Prisoner* could not have influenced Fleming and his work, the Bond themes influenced Patrick McGoohan. There is also another subtle link between Ian Fleming and the cult series of *The Prisoner*: Fleming for a time lived in Flat 22B Ebury

Street (as did Bond's nemesis Hugo Drax from *Moonraker*), part of the Pimlico Literary Institute and right next to the studio of Clough Williams-Ellis, the very man who was to create and build the incredible "village" at Portmeirion in Wales seen as the setting for *The Prisoner*. Williams-Ellis went to Trinity College in Cambridge, the same college as John Dee, and of course the infamous Aleister Crowley.

The building at 22B Ebury Street itself was like a religious shrine, or chapel residences, and Fleming had his German friend Rosie Reiss kit it out in an effect that was to be called Renaissance Jewish—dark and daunting. In a peculiar move, Fleming proposed to have the words from the German poet Novalis painted on the walls: "Wir sind im Begriff zu erwachen, Wenn wir traumen, dass wirr traumen." Nobody has commented on why he wanted this strange statement, meaning "We are about to wake up when we dream that we dream," on the wall of his apartment—although I would say that it is a very Number 6–style statement. It is not a classical statement. It makes no obvious sense of importance, unless one is aware of the subtleties of the dreaming and waking state so spoken of and admired by the secret societies and Gnostic luminaries. Could it be that Flat 22B was to Ian Fleming a religious retreat created in his own unique style? Was he aware of the hypnagogic state (the state between consciousness and unconsciousness, seen as access to the otherworld)? The evidence suggests that he was, and, more than that, it suggests he experimented, just as Walter Benjamin had.

Fleming reveals that he was very much aware that tapping into his own unconscious state was beneficial to his writing. It seems that the success with which Ian Fleming accessed his own unconscious self led to the success of *Casino Royale*, and places it in a category all by itself in the world of spy novels. John Pearson, who wrote *The Life of Ian Fleming*, claims quite clearly that *Casino Royale* was an autobiography of dreams—the dreams and unconscious world of Ian Fleming. It is in fact the result of one man's "weird obsession with himself."[7]

CHAPTER 8

A BOND HOLIDAY

In the summer of 2006 I grabbed a quick holiday with my wife and children in between the hectic preparations for a book launch, recording hundreds of radio shows, and filming for documentaries. It was the only chance I would have before flying off again for a whirlwind tour of California and more media. We had no idea where to go, but we did know that we wanted to keep it simple and stay in England. We logged on to the Internet and started searching for a nice, quiet family caravan holiday somewhere on the southeast coast of England. There was no real reason for choosing the southeast coast, other than we had never really had a holiday there. We decided on a little place called St. Margaret's Bay. Even though I was in the middle of researching Ian Fleming, I did not put two and two together and recognize the name of the place. Maybe there was some form of subliminal link, for I was to discover a remarkable coincidence.

We packed, squeezing two adults, two children, and two dogs, as well as luggage, cameras, and all manner of other things into my small Alfa Romeo. It was tight, and I feared driving too fast around the corners in case one of the doors popped open. After around five hours driving through England's congested streets we arrived at St. Margaret's Bay, to that usual nonsmiling English reception one finds irritating when one has been to the States. When I buy something in America I am generally met with a smile and an insincere "have a nice day." Whether sincere or not, I prefer the smile and nice comment to the English "what?" This is all too often accompanied by a blank or miserable expression. It really does set one on the course to a truly happy holiday and reminded me why I had taken the kids abroad the last few years. I was also reminded that Fleming had insinuated the same thing.

We opened the doors and out poured the children and dogs, along with copious other items. We decided to take the dogs for a walk and find the beach. It was a long walk across fields and down a long and damp flight of concrete stairs, but the view at the bottom was worth it. A beautiful (if stony) beach, with white cliffs on either side and a nice pub set back slightly. I noticed to the left a few whitewashed houses that looked like something from the 1920s, and gave it no more thought. We let the dogs and kids loose and watched them run off their five hours of pent-up energy as we adults and non-canines sat and sighed with exhaustion. I remember I kept saying, "Never again."

The next day I cooked breakfast and we all decided we'd take a walk down into town and see what was happening. The answer was, simply, nothing. A couple of pubs, a hotel, and a small overpriced shop were all the locals had to look forward to on a weekend. On the way to the beach I remembered seeing a sign for a museum, so we changed tack and marched off again. We were at the concrete steps and my 8-year-old daughter had reached counting higher than 100 when the sky did what it always does in summer in England: It opened up the floodgates like it was Noah's day again. We ran like mad to the museum, my wife slipping and landing like an albatross on the way. Finally, drenched and cold, we arrived at the museum—to find it closed. Luckily, next door was a small tea room with outside tables and large umbrellas. Perfect for a family with dogs. We sat down and ordered ploughman's lunch and tea all around—the dogs enjoyed the leftover cheese. It was turning out to be a typical English holiday: miserable people, rain, tea shops, and nothing to do.

But then I noticed out of the corner of my eye the shape of a man I recognized. It was a painting on the wall. There were ships from different periods, a lighthouse, and, yes, Noel Coward. As I was deep into my research on Fleming I realized that there may be something here, because Coward had been a good friend of Fleming's, and they had often lived close to each other. I couldn't have been more right, as it turned out. I asked the waitress why Noel Coward was painted on the wall, and she told me that it was because he had lived here, down on the beach. The memory from the previous day now struck me as I recalled the three or four whitewashed houses on the beach. A couple of days later, after doing some sight-seeing in the car and taking the kids swimming, we took another long stroll down to the beach. The weather was a little better, so we didn't have to run. I couldn't take my eyes off the houses, wondering which one had been home to Noel Coward. I sat for a while and opened my book on Ian Fleming while the dogs and kids chased back the waves. I searched for St. Margaret's Bay. There was nothing in the index, so I scoured the pages. I got to page 327 and found: "There were still compensations, of course, particularly the long weekends away from London with Anne [Fleming's wife] and his son Caspar at the house at St. Margaret's Bay."[1]

It turned out that Noel Coward had leased a house called White Cliffs at St. Margaret's Bay to the Flemings, and that they had spent a lot of time there. But I wanted to know which one it was, and if there was anything else I could find out. I put the book down and asked a lady who sold tea and coffee from a small hut. She wasn't sure. She knew Noel Coward had lived in one of them, but not Fleming. Then I saw an old fisherman, and he said that Fleming had definitely lived in the end house. Conclusive— or so I thought. I walked along the beach, almost forgetting my family's battle with the waves, and made straight for the end house. Then the shared back gate to the small row of houses opened and out trotted two little Scottish Terriers with tartan coats, followed slowly by an old man dressed in a silky white shirt, a cravat, and equally tartan trousers. His octogenarian hair was swept over as if to hide impending baldness, and his smile was uncommonly welcome in this land. I decided to ask him.

I walked over and he greeted me warmly, as the elder generation tends to. I asked him if he knew which house Ian Fleming had occupied.

"Yes, of course I do, my dear boy," he said with a glint in his eye. "Mine."

I was over the moon. At last, such a simple and yet difficult task had been completed!

"And do you know anything about his life here?" I pushed.

"Oh yes, there's lots of silly rumors and there's the real stuff." He started to walk with his dogs, and I followed. "The silly stuff is local folklore, like the idea that Fleming got the number 007 from the bus that used to stop at the top of the hill." I'd already checked that one out the previous day. "Utter nonsense, of course, because Ian kept the real truth of that secret—he had to." I did push, but the old man simply said that he had no idea, only that it would "give the game away, old sport."

"And what about the real stuff?" I asked as we slowly walked.

"Well, depends what you want to know," he said. "There have been a great many famous people live here over the years. Peter Ustinov used to live up there." He pointed up to the opposite cliff-face and to a beautiful set-back mansion house. "But prying eyes eventually pushed them all away."

"Well, specifically about Fleming and his time here." I pressed.

"Oh, well, he had lots of friends down, mostly literary types and posh toffs. They would swim out to sea and play about. The Flemings would walk up the hill and dance at the hotel on Saturday nights. But he also had friends around that nobody really knew of, and a lot of people thought he was still in the spying game with all the secrecy. Although others thought he was into devilish things too." The old man smiled and winked at me. "Who knows?"

I thanked him for his time and asked if he would let me use his name. "No, no, I don't want any publicity at my time of life. Take some pictures of the place if you like; I'll put the blinds down if you want."

He was a lovely old gentleman whom I shall remember for a very long time, not just because he reminded me of someone from old 1950s movies, but because of his warm and generous nature. He had confirmed to me that Ian Fleming was much more than just a writer of thrillers.

CHAPTER 9

IAN FLEMING, PART IV:
SPIRITUAL INFLUENCES

While at his Jamaican home, Goldeneye, Fleming was visited by the novelist Rosamond Lehmann, an attractive and sought-after lady at the time. In fact, the visit had been the cause of some anxiety with his then-wife, Anne, but Fleming explained that their relationship was "strictly spiritual." Indeed, this does reveal Fleming's distinctly spiritual nature, as Lehmann was certainly involved in the mystical side of life. However, there does seems to have been more to the relationship than mere spirit.

Lehmann endured mystical experiences in her later years and shared them with Fleming in Jamaica—in fact, they shared their inner and deeper esoteric thoughts one with the other. This depth of sharing was a cause of consternation to Anne, who was very much of the external world and the social graces.

Lehmann was not the only mystically inclined individual with whom Fleming associated. Another was the essayist, poet, and mystic Edith Sitwell, who I have mentioned, and who Fleming had met at a *Sunday Times* dinner for her brother Osbert, and who knew Lehmann very well. Later, Fleming was to offer to send Sitwell his translation of the lecture that Carl Jung had made on Paracelsus. As we discovered, this in itself reveals Fleming's deep understanding of the subtle psychological relationships between alchemy and the mind of man. He claimed in a letter to Sitwell that his English translation was almost as Germanic as Jung's original German, but that there were one or two original points in the speech and that had never been published.

Indeed, Sitwell wrote back saying that Jung was one of her favorites, and that she would love to see the copy, especially as it spoke of Paracelsus, another favorite. Fleming then replied and stated that he had written to Jung to ask for rights to publish the transcript, revealing that he knew the man himself and certainly understood the concepts of Jung. These concepts, as any reader of Jung will know, are ancient indeed, and speak of the true divinity within us that lies in the balancing-out of our own Self. Sitwell then suggested a book "outlining the inspiration which Mystic and Hermetic philosophers such as Paracelsus had provided to poets in general."[1] The book never happened, and if it had, then the revelations of the Bond links to the mystical world would have been revealed before now. Regardless of what did and did not get published, the fact remains that here Ian Fleming, in his links with Edith Sitwell, is revealing his true understanding of the Gnostic philosophies.

Edith Sitwell was herself a Roman Catholic mystic, and Fleming seems to have leaned more toward this element of Christianity than his home country's Protestantism. Later in his life, while spending some time in the hospital, he was visited by a close friend, Clare Blanshard, another Catholic. She was perfectly aware of his irreligious stance, and yet was surprised to find him asking her to light a candle for him in St. Patrick's Cathedral in New York. Amazingly, he later asked when the candle had been lit, and revealed that it was the same hour that his pain had lifted. This clearly demonstrates that there was a deeply spiritual element to this man—one who seemed to believe in the religious miracle.

Fleming then commissioned the cover for *From Russia With Love*, and insisted that the revolver on the front "be crossed with a rose." Those who are aware of the Christian secret society of the Rosicrucians will also be aware of the significance of this symbolic representation. Just as in the name of Bond's mother, Delacroix (of the cross), the rose crossing the revolver is a statement of hidden truths, and a subtle suggestion toward his mother's name, St. Croix-Rose. The rose has for centuries been symbolic of hidden mysteries, and has been placed upon the cover of a great many alchemical and philosophical texts, not to mention fictions holding deeper meanings, including the Bond books. Fleming was showing (to those with the eyes to see) that he was making a deep statement indeed.

Andrew Lycett, who wrote the biography *Ian Fleming*, touched on the esoteric nature of the Bond novels when he said that the notion that Ian would never reach nor strive for his full potential was an accurate one. In his truly esoteric methods, Fleming seemed to reserve his hidden talents for later Bond books, and skilfully matched his external and physical world with that of the mythical. According to Lycett, James Bond, in *Casino Royale*, is taking on the forces of evil as the heroic St. George figure, fighting on the side of virtue and a free world. He saves and beds the girl, and slays the dragon, and it is only through such epic battles that Lycett believes Fleming could understand the forces of good and bad. We have seen how Bond thinks with regard to Le Chiffre, that he was the perfect evil, by which we could judge our own goodness and that we had only ourselves to blame for the path we took.

St. George, the Dragon Slayer

Here Fleming is revealing his knowledge of the ancient systems of psychology. It is a system spoken of by Jung and Paracelsus alike, and Fleming subtly includes it within his modern works of fiction. In Buddhism and other ancient systems much the same is spoken of. Without evil in the world, how are we to know what is good? How are we to judge ourselves? Evil is a test of our resolve and fortitude, so we must be thankful of it. The Sufi mystic Rumi once said that without the rubs in life, we would never be polished. Fleming is saying exactly the same thing, and using Bond as his voice-piece. In fact, he goes further with his character as a distinct statement himself. All around Bond we find madness. Evil, chaotic individuals try to take over the world and dominate, while innocents are brushed aside like dirt. In between all of this stands James Bond, the most neutral character in the whole book. And this is the point of the esoteric perfect man—the true Gnostic must stand in neutrality, being neither good nor evil.

In *Thrilling Cities*, as we have already found, Fleming tells us that very early on in his life he got into the Jungian concepts, reading a whole host of different authors on the subjects.

The Forbes Dennises had a vast library that the young Ian Fleming could delve into, and he seems to have sponged it all up well. It was the Dennises who introduced Fleming to the Jungian psychoanalytical methods at Tennerhof in Austria, and this is one reason why James Bond's mother was to have been born in a similar place: Switzerland's mountain ranges. The other reason was that it was the birthplace of Carl Jung. It was the understanding and knowledge gained in Austria from the Swiss psychologist that was to "give birth" to the perfect man in James Bond—the new savior.

Fleming's deep interest in the philosophical world was later confirmed when, as the leader of his own publishing house, he attempted unsuccessfully to buy the publishing rights for a novel by the infamous philosopher

Evelyn Waugh

Proust, but succeeded in printing some of Evelyn Waugh's work. This connection to Waugh and Fleming's religious knowledge comes through in one particular Bond novel called *The Undertaker's Wind*, later renamed *Live and Let Die*. Even though Fleming is often thought of as irreligious his own personal spirituality, his depth of understanding of the human mind and the ancient philosophical ways cannot be denied in this book. The archrival in this case is a certain Mr. Big, who seems to have his own personal cross to bear: "Mister Bond, I suffer from boredom. I am prey to what the early Christians called 'accidie,' the deadly lethargy that envelops those who are sated, those who have no more desires."

To me, Fleming is working through the philosophies of the mind and reveals his knowledge of the Gnostic beliefs with the phrase *the early Christians*. These early Christians were of course the Gnostics. The word spoken of here, *accidie*, is indeed a word used in these early times and spoken of by the progenitors of the Gnostics—the Essene. The word is derived from the Latin *acedia*, and refers to one of the seven deadly sins—sloth. Most people believe today that sloth simply means to be lazy, but that is far from it. *Accidie* actually implies a kind of numb feeling through despair. It was Fleming's belief that the criminal was often driven to his acts by the desire to be free of accidie, and that this was due to religious indifference. In this case then, is not the irreligious Fleming stating something about everyman in the pages of those Bond novels? In fact, what Fleming is pointing to the whole time is the alter-ego of ourselves, and indeed of the main character himself—Bond. James Bond is a strong individual, with drive and virtue. The rival is equally strong, but driven by the desire to be free of boredom. This theme is an expression of Fleming's own sense of despair. He wishes to be Bond in so many ways, and so the two are distinct opposites in every way. Andrew Lycett, in *Ian Fleming*, comments that this allowed him to create and grow Bond as an antidote to accidie, giving expression to the Manichaean role in *Casino Royale* that James Bond was acting on the side of the "angels," or more to the point, that the devilish Le Chiffre was in fact *required* to exist in order for good to exist.

This is absolute proof that Ian Fleming understood well the ancient Gnostic beliefs, as Manichaeans were among the first Gnostics, and held strong to dualistic philosophy. It is now a distinct possibility, if not an established fact, that Ian Fleming would therefore move forward with this understanding of Gnostic psychology and include it within his works. His associations with Edith Sitwell and others, let alone his understanding of Jung and his translation of the lecture on Paracelsus, reveals his leanings, and so too does the subtle psychological undercurrent obvious in the Bond novels and elsewhere.

As we have seen, these Gnostic influences were strongly found in the medieval literature on King Arthur and the Holy Grail. Arthur Pendragon must unite with his Queen in order for the land to be fertile or whole. Only as the ultimate union of the divine rulers can all below be in order. Fleming understood these concepts and had read these medieval texts, later falling in love with modern writers on the subject such as Buchan. One of Fleming's later friends, the lawyer Ernie Cuneo, would say that Ian was a knight errant in search of the lost Round Table and possibly even the Holy Grail, and was therefore unable to reconcile himself to the fact that Camelot was gone, and still less, that it had probably never existed.

This peculiar statement about a man most people believed to be arrogant, selfish, and confident to the extreme is quite revealing, because it shows us another side of the man. Fleming was in search of perfection and yet knew he would never find it. In truth, Fleming was upon his own Grail Quest, and journeyed his entire life, eventually creating an alter ego in James Bond to valiantly discover the perfect state that he himself could not. He reveals this medieval esoteric plot in *Live and Let Die*, in which a fire-breathing mechanical dragon is employed, and Bond must save the innocent, naked virgin like a true knight errant. Even his favorite golf club of 30 years was called *Excalibur* after the famed sword of King Arthur.

Regarding modern texts, Fleming showed a great interest and enjoyment in the now classic novel *The Magic Mountain* by Thomas Mann, which reveals that Fleming understood the concepts of the book, which were not only darkly psychological but also intently mystical. The book discusses a wide range of concepts that would become very much part of the Fleming retinue—death, sickness, and dualism. One character used extensively in the book is Naphta, an apostate Jew who converts as a Jesuit, and is used to discuss the realms of the mystical life, despotism, and terror. The name *Naphta* comes from the Jewish name *Naphtali*, a serpent-worshiping tribe implicated in later Gnostic belief. The book is metaphysical in content and has been compared to Spenser's *Faerie Queen* and even Orwell's *Animal Farm*. Fleming's interest in such novels reveals a side of himself that no biographer has touched upon, and, like Conan Doyle with Sherlock Holmes, I believe the popular fascination with the singular character, James Bond, must have annoyed him at times.

Sex

One of the claims made about Ian Fleming by those who knew him well was that he was sexually promiscuous and enjoyed the more extreme forms of sexual pleasure. This included the claim by a close friend, Anthony Powell, that the Flemings used an incredible amount of towels because Ian used to whip his wife, Anne, into a sexual frenzy. Given Fleming's knowledge of ancient psychological methods and his understanding of the potency of sexual acts to bring on a state of high ecstasy, there is little doubt that he was enacting certain sexual rights thought by ecstatics and mystics to lead to the mystical union and the divine. In India these methods are termed the Tantric rights, and lead one into a state of sheer bliss and joy. They are linked to yoga, something with which Fleming toyed, and in which Aleister Crowley was an initiate.

In Chapter 6 we saw that Fleming was involved with the Bloomsbury Set, or, as the *Morning Post* would have it, the Bloomsbury Black Mass. Indeed, the scope of the Black Mass gatherings was quite widespread in the 1920s and '30s. In his book *Black Mass* in 1924, author J. Bricaud stated:

> It is certain, as we have shown, that the sacrilegious ceremonies, the scenes of profanation, have not disappeared. But they have lost their primitive meaning, and their psychological aspect is no longer the same. Today the followers of Satan put all their ardour into the accomplishment of what they believe to be the highest expression of sacrilege; they give themselves up to the sensual pleasures.... His disgusting saturnalias and his orgies against Nature are merely sadism.

Obviously, the author of this work was a true English Christian and was vehemently defending his faith, but the nature of the "sensual pleasures" from these times, and in fact far before and beyond, are and were still true. I believe from the evidence we have that not only were many of Fleming's associates involved in similar rites, but that he may have been himself. I had to wonder about what the elderly gentleman from St. Margaret's Bay had said: "Although others thought he was into devilish things too."

Knights Templar

In the Christian mystical undercurrents these certainly involved some form of beating. Many Christian writers accused the Gnostics of lurid sex acts, and these were always trumpeted out against the infamous

Knights Templar and the Cathar heretics. The followers of some Gnostic streams made reference to the principle of Hermes that "if you hate your body, my child, you cannot love yourself" (*Corpus Hermeticum*). The

Eastern Tantrism

belief was that one could achieve salvation, or union with the divine, through pleasure—a belief followed by the Gnostic Marcionites and Ophites, or those who worshiped the serpent. The Cainites, another Gnostic group, believed that the true friends of Sophia (wisdom) were those who rebelled against Jehovah, and so they revered Cain and the people of Sodom and Gomorrah. They proceeded with a banquet, and at the end invited their wives to "be charitable with a brother." Following orgasm, the sperm would be collected and raised towards heaven with a chant, "we offer you this gift, the body of Christ."

In a sense, what the Cainites were doing was offering the seed or source of life from the union—it was a very sacred act. These ritualistic ways are also found in Tantrism, in which it is well known both Crowley and Fleming were interested.

The concept is a simple one—that we can lose ourselves in the sexual orgy and be free of fear and unrestrained, doing things we dare not do alone. In the fusing of souls the individual loses his ego, his sense of who he is, and is united once again to the great One.

Fleming was sure to have been aware of this, and the psuedo-sexual nature of alchemy from the works of Jung and Paracelsus. Much of this would be found in Fleming's associations with the self-styled antichrist himself, Aleister Crowley, who was infamous for his use and abuse of sexual rites. And he certainly included a great many sexually deviant elements within his Bond books.

The fact is that by raising oneself into a state of pure ecstasy during ritual sex, one was releasing hormones that gave a sense of oneness with all things. It was the experience of perfect and divine union—bringing the two opposites together physically to enter the state of oneness spoken of in Gnostic literature. It also distorts a real need to be loved, for tenderness, something both Fleming and Crowley had lacked.

This union of the opposites, between the sexes, would later be given a mathematical equation in his short Bond story "The Quantum of Solace," in which the governor of the Bahamas, "who tells the story, defines the Quantum of Solace as a precise numerical notation of the amount of comfort and humanity that is necessary between two people if love is to flourish."[2]

It seems that this symmetry was to be a driving force behind Fleming's life and work: "One of the words he was always using was 'symmetry,' and in the pursuit of symmetry in his own life everything was worked out."[3]

CHAPTER 10

INFLUENTIAL PEOPLE: IN DEPTH

As we have seen so far, there were a number of influences upon the life and mind of Ian Fleming, from alchemy and mysticism to secret services, and even his family. Fleming came from a family that was expected to make waves, and, seemingly unable to make the kind of respectable surf required, he all too often stirred up a storm. In order to quiet this storm Fleming turned to the influences laid upon his shore, and these came in many guises. In order to deepen our understanding of Ian Fleming, we need to look further into the depths of this ocean of influence.

Carl Jung

The now-infamous psychoanalyst Carl Gustav Jung was from the earliest of times one of the most influential characters in Ian Fleming's life.

Jung was one of the founding fathers of modern psychology, and his importance cannot be overstated. He became famous for his statements on the "collective unconscious"—a belief, in simple terms, that we all share some form of memory or cohesion through our unconscious world—and today this concept is gaining yet more ground with modern quantum theory and "new age" beliefs.

We can see how Fleming took his literary role from the concepts of Jung in the following statement: "The artist is not a person with a free will who seeks his own ends, but one who allows art to realize its true purposes through him. As a human being he may have moods and a will and personal aims, but as an artist he is 'man' in a higher sense—he is 'collective man,' a vehicle and molder of the unconscious psychic life of mankind."[1]

Fleming was certainly a human being with "moods and a will and personal aims," but he was also an artist who had deeply understood what Jung was about, and through this element of his "true self" and his freeing up of his "collective mind" he released Bond on the world, and Bond is a character that is everyman indeed.

Among the esoteric systems that Jung researched, his first love was Gnosticism. In 1912, Jung mentioned to Sigmund Freud that he had a certain intuition that the feminine aspect of Gnostic literature (namely Sophia or wisdom) would reestablish itself on the world at large as a so-called new method of psychology. Unfortunately for Jung there was very little modern work on the subject at that time, so he had to begin a laborious trawl through ancient texts. Jung was surprised to discover that the link between the Gnostics and modern times had been broken, and he only later discovered through years of study that the link had been kept alive within alchemy: "First I had to find evidence for the historical pre-figuration of my own experiences. That is to say, I had to ask myself, 'Where have my particular premises already occurred in history?' If I had not succeeded in finding such evidence, I would never have been able to substantiate my ideas. Therefore, my encounter with alchemy was decisive for me, as it provided me with the historical basis which I hitherto lacked."[2]

To Jung, alchemy represented the historical link with Gnosticism. He said it was a continuity that existed between the past and present. Found originally within the natural philosophy of the Middle Ages, says Jung, it was alchemy that formed the bridge, on the one hand into the past and to Gnosticism, and on the other into the future to the modern psychology of the unconscious.[3]

Incredibly, Jung's lecture on Paracelcus (translated by Ian Fleming) was presented at the 400th anniversary of the death of Paracelsus, and was believed by many to be perhaps the clearest picture on record of Jung's fundamental attitude toward alchemy.[4]

According to Paracelsus (and, by default, Jung), the light of the Divine is caught or held in stasis by the Hylaster (*hyle*, "matter"; *astrum*, "star"). The only way the alchemist could release this shining light was to first reduce or break up this structure. This is the burning, torturing, and reducing spoken of in alchemy, and in the Bond novels. James Bond must undergo a constant struggle. He must be broken, or the nemesis must be destroyed in order for the Divine to be released.

Jung stated that in the process of transformation, the real, creative binaries come forth and begin interaction, or the alchemical conjunction, or union. It is this, as Jung and others have stated, that is the ultimate union and the light, which was before hidden, and can now come forth and be fulfilled.[5] The binary figures in the Bond books are the male (Bond) and female (Bond girl) characters that must unite in order to bring about the redemption, the saving, of mankind, but they must discover and do battle with the ultimate evil. The same was to be true of his so-called children's work *Chitty Chitty Bang Bang*.

In an essay by Jung entitled "The Psychology of the Transference" we find Jung employing 10 pictures to illustrate the Great Work or Opus of alchemical transformation, which were themselves found in the classic *Rosarium Philosophorum* (*Rosary of the Philosophers*). Here we find the dual natures or powers known as the king and queen undergoing a number of phase transitions in a mystical and erotic relationship, eventually uniting and forming an androgynous being.[6] Fleming simply adapts this dualistic approach, as Bond must unite with the female in order to save the day (in *Chitty Chitty Bang Bang* the mother and father are united). In fact, Jung said that literary products of highly dubious merits were often of the greatest interest to the psychologist, and he would have thought the same of Fleming's work. What Fleming did with *Chitty Chitty Bang Bang* was to take a car that was destined for the scrap heap and re-create it; he resurrected the neglected soul, and it came out flying like the alchemical phoenix from the flames of Caractacus Potts' hard labors in his mad laboratory. The car didn't fly because of a mechanical genius; it flew because of loving care, attention, and most of all, magic— the same magic that inspired John Dee to fly his magical beetle.

Jung was published in England by an esoteric publisher called Watkins, the same Watkins who, according to one of my contacts, produced astrological charts for Winston Churchill during the war, and who knew of Fleming's contacts with Aleister Crowley. Starting in April 1897, John M. Watkins first published from 26 Charing Cross, London, and produced lists for the Theosophical Society. By 1901 he had moved to Cecil Court where such literary types as W.B. Yeats, a member of the Golden Dawn, and even Fleming visited. The link between Watkins, Churchill, and astrology was important because the use of astrology would later come into play in the Fleming-Hess-Crowley scenario.

Paracelsus

We have already taken a deep look at Paracelsus, but there are other parts to the tale that reveal the Bond Code—that Fleming understood and used codes within the character and books to reveal occult significance. Paracelsus was born in 1493, and his birth sign is that of the scorpion—a favorable omen for healers, poisoners, and physicians, as we were told by Jung, and which Fleming translated. The sign is said to be that of the spy, due to the attributes of the scorpion, and it is therefore no surprise to find that the birth date of James Bond, given by Fleming, was November 11. Scorpio lies between October 23 and November 21,

The Scorpion

making Bond a Scorpio. This follows the correct astrological sign for both the spy and Fleming's earliest influence, Paracelsus.

Dame Edith Sitwell

Edith Louisa Sitwell was the firstborn child of Sir George Sitwell and Lady Ida Sitwell, born September 7, 1887. Although she was born into wealth and a seemingly content family, she was not happy in her childhood. She claimed that her parents were strangers to her from the moment of her birth, and that her father had been extreme and eccentric, while her mother had been upset by Edith's unusual features and great height.[7] She even described Lady Ida as neglectful, cruel, and often drunk, and in 1937 Edith did not attend her funeral. Strangely, her brothers, who were also writers and poets, remembered a happier childhood, and Sitwell put this down to the fact that her father had only wanted sons.

Later in life Sitwell was strongly feminist, and this ought to surprise people who claimed that Ian Fleming hated women and was a chauvinist pig. In fact, it reveals a more mature mind than many once thought—one that respected the feminine role. Sitwell was most famous for her poetry, which has been described as distinctly unique, and "this uniqueness has drawn many admirers to investigate what the true meaning is behind her important works."[8]

Among Sitwell's own influences were William Blake, the great mystic poet and artist, and indeed she herself was something of a mystic. She also admired strongly the way T.S. Eliot could see the world with different eyes.

Sitwell expounded upon the growth in consciousness, that we could see more of both ourselves and the world around us by seeing everything as a symbol of something beyond consciousness, something yet asleep, requiring awakening.[9]

Fleming respected this woman, for he saw in her work traces of the universe that he had seen in Austria. He also saw aspects of his own belief that division of the mind and heart or logic and spirit was forcing humankind into a hellhole.

Sitwell possessed a distinct reverence and understanding of the forces of nature, and many believe that her poetry is filled with the interpretations of this knowledge. Mixed ideas of time and consciousness appear throughout her work, allowing the reader to conclude that Sitwell had indeed reached an epiphany in her life. Her basic themes of heart and mind, emotion and logic, come through in the hopeless situation she highlights of lovers who will never "bond" and will therefore always remain separate due to the very nature of seeing the two elements as separate. The two are in fact one, and yet because we name we separate, and until we perceive them as one, they in fact never will be.[10] Fleming also sees this, and therefore Bond never really stays with any woman, and must move on, for the work is constant.

Sybil Leek

Another lady who supposedly knew Fleming, Sitwell, and even Crowley was Sybil Leek. Born on February 22, 1922 (it is debated that it was 1917), in Staffordshire, England, she was to eventually become one of England's most famous Witches. When only a child, the influences upon Leek were literary, profound, and somewhat mystical, as we can see by the fact that none other than H.G. Wells supposedly took her to see her very first eclipse. Her grandmother would often prepare astrological charts for the likes of Thomas Hardy, T.E. Lawrence, and Dame Edith Sitwell. Her connection with Crowley was simply that he would approach her for advice in Witchcraft and astrology matters—at least that was her claim. One of the most peculiar folktales that surrounds Leek concerns her prediction that Ian Fleming would become famous for his writing skills, and also her prediction of the date of his death.

When in the Hebrides she claimed that many top military personnel came to have their astrological charts read, including such heroes as Commander Roger Keyes—a great British Naval hero of the Second World War. She claimed that the Hebrides had a calming effect due to being cut off from warring Europe, and that protocol was dropped. And yet nevertheless she also claimed that her work was top secret, and that she occasionally saw Ian Fleming, who was dour and always busy, and appeared and disappeared unexpectedly.[11]

In the first place this seemingly innocent statement gives us a historical insight into the minds of ordinary and not-so-ordinary folk in the 1940s—that they saw no problem in having their astrological charts read, and probably believed them. This was the era of Fleming, and the one upon which he based his character of James Bond. It was natural for Fleming to include the tarot cards of Solitaire in *Live and Let Die* because they were a natural part of life to him, as astrology was to ordinary folk. So much has changed throughout such a short period. Nowadays people are almost afraid to reveal this "silly" side of their natures. Sybil Leek herself said in 1972 in her autobiography that all human beings had magic in them, and that the secret was to know how to use that magic—with astrology being a vital tool.

In fact Leek (who, with Crowley, helped Fleming with his Hess issue) claimed that as a young girl she aided Fleming in charting the Hess flight. Whether Leek actually ever met or knew Crowley personally is of some doubt. Leek's diary states categorically that she did know Crowley, who was among the many visitors to her household. He was the one she would always remember for being good-looking, with vivid and penetrating eyes, and a tremendous animal magnetism, whom she had first met when only 8 years old.

This would place the date at between 1930 and 1932, and yet Crowley was living in Germany at the time. There is in fact no supporting evidence for Leek's claims to have known Crowley, and no Fleming biographer makes any claim that she knew Fleming personally either (although that does not rule it out).

Dr. John Dee

There is no official record of the birth of John Dee, only a series of cosmic coordinates: 1527, July 13, 4:02 p.m., latitude 51 degrees, 32 seconds. This of course gives us the exact time and location (London).

Dee, the Elizabethan alchemist, astrologer, and all-around polymath, was one of the earliest known secret agents of Great Britain. It is believed that he became an agent to the queen during England's war with Spain, and he even had private correspondence with Elizabeth, signing his paperwork "007," and she signing hers "M." This evidence comes from Donald McCormick (alias Richard Deacon), who knew Ian Fleming in the secret service during the war and has since gone on to write numerous books, including a biography of Dr. John Dee. It is not outside the boundaries of truth, because even the spy and friend of Dee's, the Earl of Leicester, marked his correspondence with two dots encircled, forming a double 0, or twin eyes. The two zeros imply the eyes of the spy, and the 7 is a profoundly important number of perfection in circles of gematria. All together the number implies that Dee was not just the queen's eyes, but also her occult eyes. There is little doubt that Fleming understood gematria, as we saw in Chapter 2, when I showed that Bond is given a new code, 7777, for "it is done."

John Dee

Dee even reportedly placed "For Your Eyes Only" on his top-secret documents.* There is also some evidence that Ian Fleming was reading a biography of Dee while writing his first Bond novel, and there would be little surprise in this, as Dee would have held a fascination for a man such as Fleming who was deeply interested in alchemy, the occult, and a good spy story.

It is a fact that secret services and secret societies hold the same historical heritage, and Dee and Fleming were not averse to either. In fact, the Nazis accused British intelligence of being overrun with Rosicrucian tendencies, and John Dee is well known to have been a profound influence upon them in the 16th century—the two worlds, however divided by time, were united in creed.

Francis Yates, in her book *Majesty and Magic in Shakespeare's Last Plays*, comments, "Dare one say that the German Rosicrucian movement reaches a peak of poetic expression in The Tempest, a Rosicrucian manifesto infused with the spirit of Dee, using theatrical parables for esoteric communication?"

The time is the late 16th century, and upon the death of Edward VI, Queen Mary ascended to the throne. It was Mary who would actually invite Dee into the court circles in order to have her horoscope prepared. Dee also prepared those of Elizabeth, Mary's younger sister, who was at the time incarcerated due to the religious differences between she and Mary. Adding insult to injury, Dee then showed Mary's chart to Elizabeth, and was subsequently arrested on charges of treason and enchantment against the life of Queen Mary. He was later acquitted and found himself in Mary's entourage again—although some believe that he was acting all the time as a spy for Elizabeth. The fact that Dee was arrested with "others" suggests that he was identified as a member of a secret and Protestant cell that Mary's government believed to surround Elizabeth.[12]

In fact it appears that Dee was even using magical devices for the very purpose of national security. He was fascinated by the use of the cabala in particular as a method of encoding secret messages, and creating codes and ciphers that only those with knowledge of the occult could decipher. He was an expert in cryptography and owned several copies of Trithemious's *Polygraphia*, which was purely about codes. He also studied the works of Jacques Gohorry (*De Usu et Mysteriis Notarum*) and Jacapo Silvestri (*Opus Novum*), which he used to practice writing in cipher. When Dee made a promise to the close advisor of Queen Elizabeth,

William Cecil, that his new book would advance the "secret sciences," he was in fact referring to the art of creating codes and ciphers from an occult base. It was at this exact moment that Cecil was in fact creating the very first secret service under which Francis Walsingham would later become spymaster, and which quietly terrorized the minds of Britain's European opponents. The whole system relied heavily on codes and ciphers, and Dee was firmly placed at the very heart of it.[13]

As Elizabeth did eventually come to the throne, Dee was raised to the level of court astrologer. Similar to the later Queen Victoria, Elizabeth was fascinated by the occult, and asked Dee to decide on the date of her coronation: January 15, 1559. Amazingly, something made me wonder about this auspicious date, so I thought I would check the birth date or "crowning" of the James Bond novels. The reader should not be surprised to learn that it was in fact January 15, identified by John Pearson as the very date Ian Fleming began writing *Casino Royale*.

"Secret sciences" and "secret services" have from the start been intertwined, not least because of their links to secret societies, and so it is not difficult to see why the use of Ian Fleming and Aleister Crowley appears in the Second World War. There should be no surprise to find Ian Fleming using elements from the life and service of Dr. John Dee in his own spy novel—not least of which being the number 007—and even less surprise to find that Crowley claimed to have modeled himself on Dee.

But there is one more interesting link between Dee and Ian Fleming's books. At the age of 15 Dee went to St. John's College, Cambridge, studying 18 hours a day, and was appointed Under-Reader of Greek at Trinity College. He graduated with a BA and was made Fellow of Trinity College (the same college to which Aleister Crowley went). However, it was also at Cambridge that he first came under the charge of sorcery when he managed somehow to produce a mechanical flying beetle in the stage production of *Aristophane's Pax*. He had previously seen this done in Nuremberg: "Marvelous was the workmanship of the late days, for in Nuremberg a fly of iron, being let out of the Artificer's hand did (as it were) fly about the gates...and at length, as though weary, return to his master's hand again. Moreover, an artificial eagle was ordered to fly out of the same town, a mighty way...aloft in the air, toward the Emperor coming thither, and following him, being come to the gate of the town."[14]

It seems that Dee had for a long time had a passion for mechanical flying devices, which Fleming would use to his advantage in the children's tale of *Chitty Chitty Bang Bang*. Did Ian Fleming base Bond on Dee? We shall never truly know, but we do know that he was reading a biography of Dee at the time of writing *Casino Royale*, and we can see that Dee influenced Fleming.

Sax Rohmer

Sax Rohmer was a prolific English writer who is best known for his stories about Fu Manchu, Denis Nayland Smith, and Dr. Petrie, named after the infamous Egyptologist. He was of profound influence upon Ian Fleming, so we ought to delve a little deeper into his life and works.

Born Arthur Henry Ward to Irish parents, Rohmer actually received no formal schooling until he was 9 or 10 years old. He later changed his name to Sax Rohmer, meaning "the roaming blade" (*sax* is Saxon for "blade," and *rohmer* is Saxon for "to roam"). As a child he dreamed of being a writer, but began his working career as a clerk to a bank and then a gas company. Eventually he managed to get a job as an errand

Boris Karloff as Fu Manchu

boy for a small local newspaper, and then moved on until he became a reporter for the *Commercial Intelligence* newspaper. He claimed that his earliest influences were Egyptology and the occult, and by 1903 his first short story, "The Mysterious Mummy," was published in *Pearson's Weekly*. In 1909 he married Rose Elizabeth Knox in secret. Rose was a performing juggler with her brother Bill, and for two years the marriage was kept secret from her family. As Rose was also a self-professed psychic, Rohmer took advantage and would consult his wife. Once he asked how best he could make a living, and the infamous ouija board gave the reply C-H-I-N-A-M-A-N.

By 1910 his first book was published, entitled *Pause!*, which was a collection of short stories he had managed to get published in various newspapers. In 1913 his very first Fu Manchu novel appeared, gaining immediate success following the 1912 Fu Manchu "test" in *The Story Teller* entitled "The Zayat Kiss." The concept of this strange Chinaman leading a dangerous secret society for world domination would have had more than just a popular appeal for Rohmer. It was Fu Manchu that Ian Fleming was to base Dr. No upon, and possibly many other nefarious characters in the Bond novels. There was also alchemical influence in the Fu Manchu novels that Fleming would have picked up on and enjoyed. In the 1913 *The Mystery of Dr. Fu-Manchu*, Rohmer writes: "Greetings! I am recalled home by One who may not be denied. In much that I came to do I have failed. Much that I have done I would undo; some little I have undone. Out of fire I came—the smoldering fire of a thing one day to be a consuming flame; in fire I go. Seek not my ashes. I am the lord of the fires! Farewell."

Fu Manchu's adversary is Sir Denis Nayland Smith, a spymaster of the British secret service. The similarities between Rohmer's Fu Manchu novels and Fleming's Bond novels are almost too many.

Later, following the demise of Fu Manchu, we find Rohmer inventing Morris Klaw, who solved cases by using his dreams and visions. Rohmer's interest in the occult, similar to Fleming's, led him into the heart of it in real life when he joined the Hermetic Order of the Golden Dawn. The other members of this group were the infamous beast himself, Aleister Crowley, and W.B. Yeats, both of whom knew Fleming. Under the guidance of a Dr. R. Watson Councell, Rohmer was immersed in theosophy, mysticism, and alchemy. In his books, *Brood of the Witch Queen*, *Grey*

Face, and the *Green Eyes of Bast,* Rohmer was to push home his understanding of the alchemical, occult, and Egyptology world so popular at

W.B. Yeats

that time. Fleming, on the other hand, would not be so obvious with his occult and alchemical statements, instead hiding them inside beautifully crafted spy novels. Did Rohmer also hide subtle clues in the depths of his work? In a preface to *Apollogia Alchymiae* Sax Rohmer wrote, in 1923:

...[A]ccording to the author of the present work [this name of the proxima materia of the alchemists] is given in order to acquaint the alchemist's brother with the fact that he knows the material; it is not written for the information of the tyro. Thus, Sendivogius writes that he "intimated the art from word to word," but that his hearers "could by no means understand" him. Basil Valentine named the substance openly. Eirenaeus philalethes asserts that he could tell true writers from sophisters "by a secret character." Therefore, he must have found this word or character in the writers form whom he quotes. It is, then, for others to find, but probably not in cipher.

Sax Rohmer understood that these secrets of the alchemists had been hidden, and would continue to be so hidden, as he himself placed them within his own work. He released works such as *Masonic Symbolism* and the *Mystic Way* quite openly, though he did use the pseudonym of Arthur H. Ward. In his own name he released *A Guide to Magic, Witchcraft and the Paranormal*, in which we find infamous characters such as Nostradamus and the very first 007, Dr. John Dee.

Aleister Crowley

Born into an upper-middle-class puritanical (Plymouth Brethren) family in 1875, the young Crowley quickly became engrossed into the world of the occult. In 1895 he went to Trinity College, and by 1896 he was getting into the world of the occult, alchemy, and mysticism. It was around this time that Crowley became deeply influenced by the occultist, Freemason, and one of the founders of the Hermetic Order of the Golden Dawn, Samuel Liddell MacGregor Mathers, who was also a Rosicrucian. Later in life the two would violently disagree, and Crowley heavily criticized Mathers in his novel *Moonchild*.

Edward Kelly

With Crowley's book *White Stains*, he began a career in shocking the world, and drew scorn from the press. He joined the Order of the Golden Dawn—a society also frequented by the likes of Bram Stoker and W.B. Yeats. Crowley very soon became Grand Master, and we are told formed a homosexual relationship with Allan Bennett, another Golden Dawn member, although Crowley experts dispute the homosexual claim. Crowley declared that he wished to become a "saint of Satan," and styled himself as the "Great Beast." But he went too far, and by 1900 he was expelled

Somerset Maugham

from the order. Unperturbed by this, he set up his own order called the Silver Star, and set off to travel the world, settling in Sicily for a number of years. By now Bennett had become a Buddhist monk, and they were reacquainted in Ceylon, where Crowley was initiated into Tantrism. Later, in Paris, he met and associated with a number of people that were also close to Ian Fleming, among them Somerset Maugham. In Cairo, Crowley learned the sacred secret of the sexual union, and he eventually married Rose Edith Kelly, who died of an alcohol overdose. In the same way that Dr. John Dee listened to Edward Kelly's supposed contact with the spirit world, Crowley listened to Edith Kelly's. He went on to write *The Book of the Law*, dictated by the spirit of the minister of Horus, which he claimed to be partly in cipher and code, and which he could not understand.

Crowley continued to travel and always seemed to have an entourage of female followers. In the war, as we have already seen, Crowley was utilized, but he also directly offered Churchill a magic and infallible method of ending the war—alas, Churchill turned him down.

There are known links between Fleming and Crowley, and in my opinion there are unknown links too. How many of us throughout the course of the day, week, month, or year, record our meetings with every individual? These links, inferred and actual (whether the links with Watkins's book shop, the Second World War scenario, or frequenting the same institutions), are made more profound by the use of Crowley as a physical character for one of Bond's adversaries. They are yet deeper seen in their shared beliefs. For instance, Crowley was an initiate in Tantrism, and Fleming was well known for his peculiar (some might say perverse) sexual techniques. Tantrism is a sexual cosmogony, the union between the masculine Mahakala and the feminine Kali. They together create the great truth, the creative union bringing forth Brahma. This esoteric language was and is practiced physically, and the adept would apparently become a most sensuous and also vampiric lover—something of which those involved in Tantrism were often accused. This was the force of dissolution, the breaking up or destabilizing like the alchemical reduction. Because of these associations, Tantrism has a distinctly negative image, and yet it is one of profound strength. The naked woman is incarnated pakriti (neutrality) and should be worshiped as the secret of nature itself. The union of the male and female is the most sacred of acts.

I asked one of today's leading experts on Crowley, O.H. Krill, for a statement on how he saw Crowley and his links to Fleming. This is what he said, reprinted exclusively with permission:

> Crowley is the most misunderstood of all. The only real secret the Golden Dawn had was that the orgasmic level is to be used to create and conjure. More or less, they were not true magicians and did not truly work to achieve their goals, which is why he left them in disgust. No such organization or collective holds a candle to the Crowley, the true enigma of modern times. With reference to tantra, this is what Crowley the magician was really doing as opposed to [sex] Tantra, which is more for gluttonous pleasure-seekers. Crowley was not this, although he did fall to drugs in the end, but only seeking something more. He never wasted his time or energy, always working to make the next thing happen, the next level of himself. He used to climb huge mountains for Christ's sake, nobody speaks of this; he was an expert

mountain climber, the tops. Fleming...tapped into certain Crowley conjure mechanisms to help create characters and stories indeed. Many other great achievers probably pimped Crowley as well. Crowley is a Rosicrucian among other things as well. Again, people never talk about that, ONLY the national inquirer of the day, headlines Journalism. This is why Crowley could care less, he had this power over them because he could play their game and really not care either way. He was guilty of toying with some sloth-like humans, his greatest disdain.

Maxwell Knight

Charles Maxwell Knight was born in Mitcham, Surrey, in 1900. He spent time in the Royal Navy and is infamous for his right-wing notions. In 1924 he joined the British Fascisti—an organization established to counter the rise of the Labor Party—where he quickly became the director of intelligence. This work brought him to the attention of Vernon Kell in MI5. By 1925, Knight had been recruited to work for the Secret Service Bureau, and was placed in charge of B5b, the unit responsible for keeping tabs on political subversion. In the following years he wrote two spy thrillers, played drums in a jazz band, and was a fellow of the Royal Zoological Society, as well as recruiting numerous young spies to the fold. One of his agents was Ian Fleming, and it is believed (because it has been promulgated) that the code "M" is based upon Maxwell. Another agent he employed was Joan Miller, a member of various right-wing and anti-Semitic organizations. Miller's autobiography was published in opposition to the wishes of MI5 by her daughter in 1986, entitled *One Girl's*

War: Personal Exploits in MI5's Most Secret Station. In it, Miller points out the occult goings-on and sexual exploits within the secret service.

He claimed that Maxwell Knight's first wife died in the Overseas Club following some bizarre occult misadventure involving the infamous Aleister Crowley, but failed to delve too deeply into the affair. Black

Maxwell Knight

magic, he said, did not hold any fascination for him, but he accepted Knight's interest in it, hoping that it was for purely academic reasons. Apparently, when Miller tore up a photograph of Crowley that Knight had kept because he believed it to be unlucky, Knight simply responded with a laugh.

There is little wonder that the Germans, during the Second World War, believed that it was the British Intelligence who were being run by occult groups, and Himmler even named the Rosicrucians as the main group behind MI5. There is little wonder that Rosicrucian elements keep cropping up in the life of Ian Fleming, if the secret services were in fact closely connected. According to author Peter Levanda in his book *Unholy Alliance*, Maxwell Knight was in fact a disciple of Crowley, and Miller's autobiographical account seems to substantiate this claim. It has always been the case, and was also in the time of Dr. John Dee, that secret services and secret societies mingle; it seems this was true in Fleming's time, and this must therefore have influenced him.

According to Michael Howard,[15] Maxwell Knight appealed to Crowley to learn more, and stated that Crowley was in appearance similar to that of an Oxford Don. Although Knight and Fleming's friend, the author Dennis Wheatley, stated that the interest in Aleister Crowley was purely academic, the facts will never be known. Dennis Wheatley did make an excellent living out of books on the occult and Witchcraft, but Maxwell Knight did not. Maxwell Knight is also believed to have spoken out against involving Aleister Crowley in the Hess affair—for reasons we are not told.

The circumstances have to speak for themselves, because none of the main characters speak with one voice, if they speak at all. British Intelligence was smothered with people involved in the occult, and even the Germans believed secret societies to be involved with the Rosicrucians (see Appendix A). There may be more than one reason for Ian Fleming to have joined SIS at the start of the war, and these reasons may indeed have been his association with secret societies and his knowledge of the occult.

Other Characters

During his time at Durnford boarding school near Swanage, Ian Fleming announced that he had become deeply interested and influenced by such characters as John Buchan, who wrote *39 Steps*. It is well known that Buchan was interested in the occult and mysticism, and in his own *Pilgrims Way* he told of a revelation that transcended human expression, and how he felt the universe as One. Mystical language and coded methods can be gleaned from his many works, and it is possible that Fleming later on understood these.

Another influence was that of Edgar Allan Poe, who was called an American Gnostic by author Harold Bloom due to his metaphysical and mystical leanings. Poe was also a great influence on the creator of Sherlock Holmes, Sir Arthur Conan Doyle, who himself influenced Fleming. While at Durnford, Fleming also spoke of his love of Robert Louis Stevenson, the infamous writer of *Dr. Jekyll and Mr. Hyde*, which of course is a Manichean Gnostic analogy from start to finish—literalizing the inner conflict between light and dark within all of us. It is little understood just how rife these supposedly heretical concepts were in the late 19th and early 20th centuries, and it was into this literary and mystically inclined age that Ian Fleming bloomed.

Edgar Allan Poe

We have seen now the vast influences known to have affected Ian Fleming. There are a great many elements that are not recorded, and I feel sure that in the course of time and with the deaths of certain individuals, more will come out. Concluding that Fleming was a member of any specific secret society such as the Rosicrucian Brotherhood is difficult, but the inference is definitely there with his numerous contacts and links. The only element left to us now is to see some of the codes that Ian Fleming placed into his Bond novels.

CHAPTER 11

THE BOND CODE IN NAMES

Throughout this book we have seen the influences brought to bear upon Ian Fleming. We have seen how ancient and mystical Gnostic concepts influenced his overarching plot themes, and how psychoanalytical concepts were introduced within his Bond books as methods of self-help and possibly of passing on the torch of light. Occasionally I have hinted at or explained the meaning behind certain names. The following (and final) chapter before my conclusion outlines these names and more, and within the meanings we will see the Bond Code at work.

Mr. Big

One of the aliases of Mr. Big is Gallia, which is the name of a metallic substance discovered by the French 19th-century alchemist Paul Emile

Lecoq de Boisbaudan, meaning "France" from the Latin *gallus* for "le coq" (cock crows at sunrise)—he named the discovery after himself, although for patriotic reasons he denied this in 1877. He was also known (in the film) as *Kananga*, a Voodoo and Angolan term for "water used to purify."

Mr. Big was indeed the nemesis of both Bond and Fleming, having almost the exact opposite lifestyle of both, and yet suffering from the same disease as Fleming himself: "He didn't drink or smoke and his only Achilles heel appeared to be the chronic heart disease which had, in recent years, imparted a greyish tinge to his skin" (*Live and Let Die*).

Mr. Big was the dark side to the light of James Bond: "The rumor had started that he was the Zombie or living corpse of Baron Samedi himself, the dreaded Prince of Darkness" (*Live and Let Die*).

Baron Samedi

In *Live and Let Die* Mr. Big runs the cult of Baron Samedi: "He is...the head of the Black Widow cult and believed by that cult to be the Baron Samedi himself." His name meaning simply the "Baron of Saturday," Samedi is one of the Loa or spirits of Voodoo, often referred to as mysteres or invisibles, akin to angels in Christianity. They are also known strangely as *Bondye* ("bon Dieu" or "good God"), who exist between humanity and the creator. They exist in the twilight world between waking and sleeping, between this world and the next, and in *Live and Let Die* Mr. Big is "believed by that cult to be the Baron Samedi himself." This places Bond's, and therefore Fleming's, nemesis between himself and God, and he must overcome this aspect in order to reach the Divine. In fact several Loas exist, but Fleming chose Samedi out of them all, as if there were something recognizable about him, which may have been his specific Bond-style attire of a black tuxedo—dressed for death. Samedi is also a very sexual Loa with great phallic symbols used to represent him as he stands on the doorway to the next realm—bridging the gap.

Baron Samedi

Hugo Drax

In *Moonraker*, Fleming casts his hero against Hugo Drax, a self-made millionaire. This is of course in complete opposition to Fleming himself, who never really needed money, and yet did need it to prove his worth to his expectant mother. Drax is all that is hateful about Fleming's own character—torn and ripped apart by the desire to please his mother, impress friends, and be someone himself, rather than the younger brother of a famous writer or the son of a hero.

The etymology of Hugo reveals that it is a form of Hugh, which is a Teutonic word for "heart," "mind," or "spirit." Drax is a form of dragon. Originally he was known as Graf Hugo von der Drache, implying a German noble lineage. In this way Fleming is implying that Hugo Drax is of the noble order of the dragon, an ancient order entrenched in Gnostic belief similar to the Knights Templar, and that he is on the "wrong" side—German, from where influences such as the Rosicrucians and the Golden Dawn were derived. There is also a link here to the name of Patrick McGoohan's *Dangerman*, the spy series that gave rise to *The Prisoner*, which was itself full of esoteric, alchemical, and occult inferences, and of course spoofed Bond. The main character in *Dangerman* is seen by most *Prisoner* fans to be the same character as Number 6, although in *Dangerman* he is given a name: John Drake (drake is "dragon").

Auric Goldfinger

The rival to Bond in *Goldfinger* is Auric Goldfinger. We do not have to go far with this name to see the not-so-subtle alchemical references: *Auric* is indeed a term used by alchemists for the gold made from lead, the divine substance from the base material. The goldfinger is of course a compound name of gold and finger, and was of Jewish origin. It was the finger that could transmute or the finger turned to gold due to working with it all day. Here we have a tradition many hundreds of years old, for the Jews and their mystical kabbalah were often blamed for introducing alchemy into Europe. It is the fool and cheat who believes that real gold can be made from the prime material, and Goldfinger is revealed as the fool and cheat by Bond on numerous occasions for this kind of deception.

Ernst Stavro Blofeld

As the nemesis of James Bond, Blofeld is also the nemesis of Ian Fleming, and Fleming makes this point obvious when he gives Blofeld the exact same birthday: May 28, 1908. He is even an expert in engineering and radios, having studied at the Warsaw Technical Institute, something at which Ian Fleming himself was to prove useless. The name Blofeld means "blue field," a swipe at his own blue blood rampant in the field, like heraldry.

At the start of the Second World War Blofeld spies for the Germans, just as Fleming had been a spy for the British, and Blofeld has a network of spies, which he calls Tartar, after the Greek Hell. Blofeld sets up the now infamous SPECTRE agency after the war, and begins in Thunderball to steal two nuclear warheads from the British government in order to extort £100 million. Blofeld is in fact such a threat to Bond that he even kills Bond's wife, Tracey.

The name is also revealing in a psychological way. *Ernst* is Teutonic for "earnest," and *Stavros* is Greek for "victor," and so he is the "'earnest victor." In *Thunderball*, Blofeld is aided by the underling Emilio Largo, whose name means the "moving flatterer."

As the creator of SPECTRE, Blofeld is in reality the spectre of Ian Fleming that looms ever present within his divided mind.

Marc-Ange Draco

The father of Tracey (Teresa) Bond (and therefore the father-in-law of James Bond), Marc Draco was the head of a powerful crime syndicate in Italy, and Bond uses this contact to get to his nemesis Blofeld. Draco of course is "the dragon," and so he is the "mark of the dragon." Bond therefore married Tracey (born Teresa) Draco—the female dragon. This incredibly follows tradition for the savior-styled man of ages past, as I have shown in other books. King Arthur of English myth was himself the Pendragon and married the Queen of Serpents, Guinevere, just as Solomon was to marry Sheba, the Queen of Serpents. Adam is the consort of Eve, whose name means "female serpent," and this pattern is found across the world as a union of the wisdom and power of the serpent/dragon. Fleming is not only revealing how widely read he is, but he is also showing his understanding of the so-called serpent fire or solar fire of the alchemists. The truth, the illumination, and the discovery of the self shall, we are told by our ancestors, only be discovered via the union of the twin serpentine energies—symbols of physical energy and internal psychological processes of reduction and rebirth, of balance and wisdom.

Scaramanga

This is "The Man with the Golden Gun" who has three nipples, played excellently by Christopher Lee (a relative of Ian Fleming and of royal descent) in the film version. Again, this assassin is a nemesis of Bond with style and panache, and so there is little surprise to find that his name has a deeper meaning, regardless of the tired old "standard" reasoning touted by Fleming. Scara is Etruscan/Italian/French for "inwards," and manga is a "caricature," and so Scaramanga is a "caricature of what is within." It is an incredible use of etymology that Fleming would have obviously been cautious of revealing, for the caricature was of his own darkness.

To discover what is within and to then take action against the negative, oppressive elements of oneself is exactly the work of the alchemists and philosophers. Bond must take this shadow of himself/Fleming—a worthy assassin—and destroy him.

Another meaning of *Scaramanga* is also quite telling: The *scaramangum* is actually Italian for a "mantle covering the whole body," and therefore Scaramanga also means "to masquerade."

Miss Solitaire

Solitaire is the precognitive tarot card reader working for Mr. Big in *Live and Let Die*. She is the representation of the spiritual side of us all that must be united with the logical. She is solitary because the evil one—Mr. Big—will not allow sexual union for fear of losing power. This is true of us all, and it is something about which Fleming spoke openly. By uniting with the feminine principle, Bond is actually breaking the divisive spell of Mr. Big, and thus succeeds.

Felix Leiter

Felix Leiter is the CIA agent who helps Bond on numerous occasions. Leiter is Germanic in origin, and means "leader," "ladder," "conductor," or "manager." Felix is Latin for "lucky" or "happy." Felix Leiter is therefore the happy leader or helper.

Vesper Lynd

Vesper Lynd is the Russian double-agent who is sent to spoil Bond's fun in *Casino Royale*. Vesper is Latin for "evening star," from the Proto-Indo-European wespero for "evening," and gave rise to the term *vespers* for evening prayers. Lynd has several meanings, from "spring," "bird," and "lime tree" to "to bear," as a child. Vesper Lynd appears therefore to mean the birth of evening—it is the twilight period, birthing night, when darkness appears.

Gettler

Gettler is a SMERSH agent who finally catches up with Vesper Lynd in *Casino Royale* and scares her so much that she commits suicide. What is it about this man that is so scary? Maybe it's his name, for it means "God."

Tiffany Case

Tiffany Case is the Bond girl from *Diamonds Are Forever*. Tiffany is from the Greek Theophania, and means quite simply "manifestation from God." Taken as a whole, the etymology of Tiffany Case is something similar to "the manifestation of God fallen below," where case from Old French, Latin, and Proto-Indo-European, is "to fall."

Darko Kerim Bey

Seen in *From Russia With Love* as the head of the British Secret Service in Turkey, the name means "gift" (darko), "great wonderment" (kerim), and "one with authority" (bey).

James Bond

Why did Ian Fleming choose this ordinary name for an extraordinary spy? The official story states that Fleming was reading a book on bird-watching by a certain James Bond at the time of writing the first novel; however, with the fact that Fleming spent such a lot of time hiding meaning behind the other characters in his books, there can be little doubt that there would also be a deeper meaning to the name of the main character.

Sean Connery, the first 007 in film

This puzzle bothered me for some time. There were several layers I could apply. But one Sunday afternoon I decided to watch *Thunderball* with Sean Connery as the hero. The film begins with Bond at a funeral, and there before us is the monograph JB. This immediately struck my senses because this is a very Masonic monograph. The Freemasons claim to uphold the secrets of our sacred past, and their greatest symbols are the twin pillars of Joachim and Boaz, often depicted as JB. These twin pillars come from the Temple of Solomon, and were the entrance portal to the temple itself—one had to go between them to enter the inner sanctum. They represent perfect balance and the neutral state one must be in to access the true Divine.

Of course, there are other elements to the name: James, for instance, is the brother of Jesus, and *bond* is another term for "covenant," as in the Ark of the Covenant or Jesus as the "new" covenant. The character of Bond also has a scar or mark on his left shoulder, known in esoteric circles as the Mark of Cain, and is a symbol of the chosen and also of the serpent. James Bond is named, initialled, and marked out perfectly, as any good cipher expert would do.

James Bond was given another name when he was reborn or resurrected in *You Only Live Twice*: Taro Todoroki, which means "firstborn thunder," and thunder is symbolized by the dragon in Japanese, so Bond is the firstborn dragon. As we have seen throughout this book, the dragon or winged serpent was utilized across the world for many reasons, but in Japan it was a symbol of good, strength, and power. To be resurrected as the firstborn dragon was a great alchemical honor indeed.

Looking at the numerology of the name we find that James Bond is highly sensitive, promotes cooperation and diplomacy, and makes everyone feel safe and appreciated. Flexible and passionate, the name promotes adaptability and survival against all odds. The name indicates understanding, compassion, and intimacy, and tends to draw support with tact and subtle persuasion rather than force and confrontation. Having an intuitive ability to avoid land mines and pitfalls, and a strong sense of balance, this name promotes a careful and competent decision-making process.

The Mark of Cain and the Shaman

There was a mark known to have been placed upon Cain by God to set him aside for murdering Abel and lying. It is part of the occult and Gnostic belief system that Jehovah was not the real God, but instead it was Lucifer. One of the groups said to have marked themselves as a sign of devotion to Cain were the Cainites. This mark is a continuation of a concept spoken of among Shamans and seers for centuries—that the true adept, or the one who could access the Divine, would be marked, probably on the right hand or shoulder.[1] The red cross of the Knights Templar, placed upon white linen on the shoulder, is thought by some to be in remembrance of this mark of Cain, due to their heretical beliefs. These concepts were understood by the Rosicrucians and the Freemasons, both of whom influenced Fleming. Not surprisingly, the distinguishing features of James Bond are a red scar on his left shoulder and the back of his right hand. The mark on his hand was made in *Casino Royale* when SMERSH agents set Bond free after marking him with an S for "spy." The S is Cyrillic, from the language of St. Cyril, a devoted Christian who gave himself up to the pursuit of heavenly wisdom at the age of 7. Therefore, James Bond bears the symbol or code of one who is in pursuit of heavenly wisdom, beginning at the age of that all-important number, 7.

Q and 007

Q in all likelihood stands for quartermaster, the man who issues the tools of the trade. It is also the term given to the hypothetical source material for the New Testament from the German quelle, meaning "source," and termed the "Q Document." This concept was new during Ian Fleming's youth, and grew in popularity as he grew. If Fleming saw Bond as a kind of savior, then Q would be his source material.*

Another interesting connotation is the ratio scientists discovered for the mathematical equations of gravity (the "thing" that holds everything together): "Q." All of the wonderful new discoveries in the realm of particle physics and astronomy were really taking off in Ian Fleming's time, and we know that Fleming met Albert Einstein and was incredibly impressed by him. This would have been something of a coincidence had I not been reading *Just Six Numbers* by Martin Rees for a documentary I was making on quantum physics. The six numbers spoken of are the numbers that make up the nature of our universe, and it is these numbers that were worked out and discovered mostly during Fleming's period. If any of these numbers were out of tune—bigger or smaller—often by just a fraction, then life would not be as we know it; these numbers are in fact the deep forces that shape our universe. One of these numbers or ratios is called Q (1/100000), but there is another that has a strong and indivisible relationship with this ratio, known as ε. Here is an extract from Martin Rees's book:

> Accounting for the proportions of the different atoms—and realizing that the Creator didn't need to turn 92 different knobs—is a triumph of astrophysics. Some details are still uncertain, but the essence depends on

just one number: the strength of the force that binds *[i.e. a Bond!]* together the particles (protons and neutrons) that make up an atomic nucleus.... So the fuel that powers the Sun—the hydrogen gas in its core—converts 0.007 of its mass into energy when it fuses into helium. It is essentially this number, ε, that determines how long stars can live.[2]

Incredibly, what scientists discovered were two numbers that helped to bond the universe together—gravity and ε—Q and .007!

Albertus Magnus

Q was a perfect ratio—the gravity (albeit weak) holding all things in their place. The ε as .007 could not be .001 more or less for fear of all life coming apart or crunching into a heavy ball. They are the perfect union. "The actual mix of elements would depend on ε, but what is remarkable is that no carbon-based biosphere could exist if this number had been .006 or .008 rather than .007."[3]*

Was Ian Fleming making a subtle astrophysicist joke? James Bond as 007 was the number that "binds" together; a number used by Dr. John Dee, a mathematician, alchemist and astronomer—an astrophysicist of the 16th century. There is another peculiar coincidence, and when one has too many coincidences one has to ask—are they all accidental? The coincidence in this instance comes from the TV series called *The Prisoner* that we touched on in Chapter 7. One of the famous elements of this program was the signage and typeface, or font. It was an adaptation of a font entitled Albertus, altered according to McGoohan's "taste" and renamed Village. Albertus is named after the alchemist Albertus Magnus. The subtle changes, almost indiscernible to most people, revolve around the E, which was changed to form the symbol for the number .007. This is how the title appears in Village font:

The Prisoner

Note that the E is now in the Greek formula.* Because *The Prisoner* came after the creation of James Bond, and because it cannot have influenced Ian Fleming, the inference is that it could have influenced Patrick McGoohan, who created, wrote, and starred in the series, and who has always remained tight-lipped and mysteriously smug about the real meaning behind the show. McGoohan was asked to play Bond, but refused on the grounds of having personal problems with another member of the crew.

APPENDIX A

TERMS

There are many terms used throughout this book (and some not used but nonetheless relevant) that may bring deeper insight into who and what we are, and the ancient concepts alluded to by Ian Fleming and those people influential upon him. The following terms are defined here as aids and guides to that deeper understanding.

Ablution

An alchemical term for washing a solid with a liquid. However, the real meaning is to purge oneself of those things that cause suffering, such as desire or ego.

Agartha

This Tibetan word means "the underground kingdom placed at the center of the earth, where the king of the world reigns." It is used extensively to imply the true center. This is a device utilized by the followers of the enlightenment experience for the central aspect needed to gain illumination.

Alchemy

Al or *El* is "God" or "Shining." *Khem* or *Chem* is from the Greek root *kimia*, and means "to fuse." Therefore *alchemy* means "to fuse with God or the Shining"—to be enlightened.

Basically it was a cover for Eastern traditions, which ran diametrically opposed to the Church of Rome, and was therefore heretical. This is the reason for the obvious crossover of meaning hidden behind the subtle language of the alchemists. It was brought into Europe via the teachings of Geber (Jabir ibn Hayyan, AD 721–815), among others. In later years psychoanalyst Carl Jung concluded that the alchemical images he was finding emanating from his subjects' dreams and thoughts explained the archetypal roots of the modern mind and underscored the process of transformation.

Alkahest

This is the alchemical term for the power that comes from above and allows or makes possible the alchemical transformation. Sometimes translated as "universal solvent," it is the concept of transmuting material (or mental) elements into their purest forms. It is in essence the concept of revealing the hidden and true nature of humankind, which is the real "gold" of these arcane philosophers.

Anima and Animus

Terms developed by psychologist Carl Jung, springing from the alchemists' term for the soul. The anima is the feminine nature of the male, and the animus is the male nature of the female. It was Jung's concept of the bisexual nature of us all, and a reflection of the "biological fact that it is the larger number of male (or female) genes which is the decisive factor in the determination of sex."[1]

The anima and animus he believed manifested as archetypes in the dream or fantasy state, where the man's feelings were his feminine side and the woman's thoughts were her male side.

Archetype

Appearing as early as the mid-16th century, the word *archetype* is derived from the Latin *archetypum*, from the Greek *arkhetypon*, meaning "first molded."

The psychological archetype (as opposed to the scientific) is the generic impulse or idealized object or concept. The words *stereotype* and *epitome* are often used as examples of the simplified archetype. It is the definition of a personality; for instance, Father Christmas is an archetype seen in many cultures under different names and guises— all relating to one core archetypal concept.

Archetypes are used to analyse individuals, to ascertain their inner realities; that is, what is going on inside their unconscious states. The reason that this is so successful is that archetypes seem to be universal parts of the human unconscious mind—manifested in various ways, such as in the savior figures of Christ or Horus. These archetypes are within us all because they developed alongside our consciousness and conscious interpretations of the world around us—they are part of the whole human evolutionary life in the same way that an arm or a leg is.

Often these archetypes manifest in stories, fables, myths, and today in popular fiction. Indeed, most modern archetypal figures, such as Robin Hood or Superman, can be found in parallel tales thousands of years ago. The most popular of these is the hero, a tale found related to the solar divinity and the resurrecting capabilities of the sun.

Atman

This is the true inner reality, the Spirit or the "Son of God" element within each one of us. Alchemists say that the Atman does not die, is without end of days, and is absolutely perfect.

Baqa'

A Sufi term referring to the Divine Attribute of Everlastingness. It is opposite to Fana' or Passing Away. When the Sufi reaches the state of Fana' he is leaving himself behind, and then only the Divine Self remains.

Bipolar

This is often known as manic-depressive disorder, and can cause mood swings and extremes of energy. These symptoms of the bipolar individual are more severe than the ordinary mood swings most people have, and they often result in broken relationships, loss of employment, and poor performance. The typical onset of a bipolar disorder begins around the teens or early adulthood—although this is not always the case. Unless properly diagnosed, the individual is often unaware of the disorder.

Consciousness

Consciousness is the state we are in right now, because we are aware and perceptive. When we are no longer aware of things or thoughts, then we are unconscious—although our unconscious state may very well be aware of what is happening around us. The conscious state is what we assume to be us, to be the real me and you, but this is only half of the coin, and the rest of our real self is hidden within the unconscious world. When we think of who we are, we immediately assume it to be the person we envisage in our conscious state. Using archetypes and associations discovered in dreams, psychologists tap into the hidden part of our mind. Some philosophers break consciousness down into experiential (phenomenal) consciousness and abstract (access) consciousness.

Consciousness is definitely part of the brain function, as we may lose limbs and still remain conscious, but the question of whether we are conscious after death has always played upon the minds of the greatest thinkers, with few conclusions being reached. Breaking the structure and actions of the brain down into hard science reveals that it is an organic structure enlivened by electromagnetic energy of wave-particle transmissions across neural networks. That is, our conscious or unconscious thoughts are waves and particles created by energy escaping from one atom and entering the next. In fact, this is the same as the very structure of our universe, and so our thoughts are very much in line with the greater universe—a concept said by Prof. James Gardner to be intelligent at the subatomic level. Waves may reduce and die, but particles may not, and within those thought particles we have information stored during our entire lifetime, which may be entangling with particles in the greater universe in a "DNA feedback loop." In essence, there may yet be found in quantum physics what the philosophers have been searching for: life after death. (See my book *Gateway to the Otherworld*, New Page Books, 2008.)

Dharma

An Eastern word, *dharma* is the innermost nature of every individual, and is the true Being. It is the meaning of life. Man is not acting to his full ability if he does not know his dharma.

Dream

A dream is an experience of visions and sounds during sleep, and is a doorway into our unconscious self. Within our dream state we often have experiences that would be unlikely in the conscious world, and these will involve archetypes and representations of who we are (or believe we are). Lucid dreaming, on the other hand, is the conscious experience of the dream, and can be most disturbing or indeed enlightening for the person experiencing it. Many spiritual seekers claim to have mastered lucid dreaming and thereby claim access to the otherworld of the mind and another realm entirely. In fact, the two extremes, that dreams are reflections of our unconscious self or that they are mirrors to the world of the divine, are both aspects understood as gnosis—the mystical experience of the divine in the self.

Dreams are powerful devices for the mind. They help us come to terms with issues that have occurred during the day, and may be a restructuring of the neural pathways of which we are only partly sometimes conscious—a kind of re-filing or defragmentation of the hard drive.

Some philosophers believe that the dream state is the access to humankind's past, as our genetic history may be "remembered" as our evolution progressed.

Ego

Psychologically, the ego is the destructive part of ourselves, causing suffering through desires, which lead to us making decisions about our lives, which are at odds with the inner reality of divinity. We can only eradicate the ego (or egos) by realizing its effect upon us and our errors because of the force of it. Once we realize we have the ego or egos, we can set about removing it/them. Buddhists teach that we need to be free from the suffering caused by this element of our lives, and give us a clear and distinct Eightfold Path to Enlightenment (which is the release):

▶ Creative comprehension.

▶ Good intentions.

▶ Good words.

▶ Total sacrifice.

▶ Good behavior.

▶ Absolute chastity.

▶ Continual fight against the Dark Magicians (alter egos).

▶ Absolute patience in all.

Follow this path and be free from the sufferings caused by opposites such as bad words and deeds, and giving in to impatience.

Fana'

The ego death or the passing away of the self, leaving behind the Divine Self in Sufi tradition. The final element of fana' is the fana' al-fana', which simply means "the passing away of the passing away." This is the stage when the Sufi is no longer even aware of having "passed away."

Haqiqah

The Sufi word for "inner reality," coming from the root *al-haqq*, which means "truth." Therefore, the inner reality of ourselves is truth, and truth is our inner reality, which can only be gained by fana' or the passing away of the self (ego).

Insan al-kamil

The perfect man, the pure and holy one, or the universal man. This term is used in Sufism for the one who is a fully realized human being.

Jnana

A Sanskrit term meaning simply "to know," and related to gnosis. Specifically, the term refers to the enlightenment of the consciousness, or wisdom from within. The equivalent Tibetan word *yeshe* means "to know the prime knowledge that has always existed," and this reveals the real meaning of the terms *gnosis* and *jnana* as that inherent human and inner wisdom we can find by eradicating the ego.

Monad

"The self," from Latin *monas*, meaning "unity," or "a unit." Man and woman are the physical manifestations of the spiritual monad, and the divine monad resides in each of us as the Father, Son, and Holy Spirit. The objective of the monad is said to be self-realization.

Monism

The belief that everything in the universe is made of the same thing, and that metaphysically all things are one and unified.

Nirvana

A Sanskrit word meaning "extinction." It is not heaven in the Western sense of the word, but instead a state of being, free from Kilesa (contaminants of the mind). These contaminants are not just materialisms, but also the deadly sins such as lust, hate, and anger. Free from these constraints one is in a state of bliss, hence nirvana. But this freedom must be total and consistent, which is the realm of nirvana, for transitory freedom (going back to Kilesa) is not true nirvana.

Buddha said that nirvana was deathlessness, and the highest state of being, derived from good and right living. The opposite of nirvana is samsara, which is ignorance or clinging to Kilesa (the contaminants) in accordance with dharma.

To the early Christians known as Gnostics, nirvana was no different from true gnosis or knowledge. It is neither coming nor going, neither up, nor down, but perfect, peaceful neutrality from all contaminants.

The traces of this concept can be found emerging from India into Semitic (and Islamic in the concept of Baqa'), Egyptian, and later Christian thought in Gnosticism, and then into medieval Europe via the hidden language of the alchemists. Alchemy was not about turning lead into gold, but burning off the contaminants of the mind and emerging, phoenix-like, in a state of true enlightenment. Opposed by the controlling elite within the Catholic Church, alchemy was frowned upon, and yet allowed to continue, as those in authority knew full well that the ordinary man would not understand the arcane language.

Persona

Derived from the Latin for "mask," a persona is a character one plays, and not the real self. It is also known as the alter-ego (Latin for "the other I"). We present our persona to the world as if it were truly us, and yet our unconscious and subconscious selves realize that this is a lie, and so we torture our inner selves with illusion. We take on the persona of others, such as when we are greatly influenced by an individual who may be a father or mother figure or an archetypal hero with which we associate. It is simply our way of dealing with the world, and is derived from evolution itself—the learning ability within each of us in order to better survive. There are issues with this drive, though, especially when we do not realize what we are doing and eventually end up with a million different personas with which we confuse the outside world as well as ourselves. People actually end up believing that the persona or character they are playing is truly themselves, and lose all sight of who they really are.

Psychosis

Several times in this book I have mentioned psychosis, so I needed to include it here because it can be misinterpreted. It is in fact a simple, generic term for a mental state in which thought, perception, and reasoning are impaired. Episodes of psychosis can bring about altered states of consciousness, hallucinations, and lucid dreaming, and cause people to have delusional beliefs. In this way, most of the world is psychotic.

Paradoxically, although the individual suffering from psychosis has strange visions (and therefore half the prophets of religion were psychotic) and altered states of awareness, he or she fails (and refuses utterly) to see the strangeness of his or her own actions and perceptions. This demonstrates a complete lack of insight, so the claim that the "kundalini is enlightenment" can be completely wrong, because instead of achieving an enlightened state away from the contaminants of the mind, the individual instead is distancing him- or herself from reality. Most psychotics, and a great many people who have had psychotic (or sporadic kundalini) experiences, end up distancing themselves from others in society, and have impaired social behavior. It is in fact a severe mental illness and is associated with bipolar disorder and schizophrenia. People who are psychotic will often have deep mood swings, persecutory syndrome, and depression, and the causes can be varied, from drug and alcohol abuse to brain damage, and even the kundalini (an electromagnetic, chemical, and biological effect within the brain). Research has shown that people with tendencies towards psychosis show increased activation in the right hemisphere of their brain. This location is responsible for our emotions, beliefs, and paranormal attachments to explanations other people find ludicrous. The same activity in the right hemisphere has been found in people who have mystical experiences and report paranormal activity such as ghosts and UFOs. It may be simply that people who have different viewpoints from the norm are not psychotic, but that they think using their right and intuitive hemisphere as opposed to the logical and ordered left hemisphere (used for constructs of mathematics).

Rosicrucians

The Rosicrucians are a brotherhood of scholars, alchemists, and esoteric proponents formed in or around the 17th century. They were bound together informally, so the legend that surrounds their origins and activities is profound. On a poster that appeared in Paris in 1622 we read: "We, deputies of the principal college of the brothers of the Rose-Cross, are making our stay both visible and invisible in this town...in order to draw men, our equals, from deadly error."

Some have seen in this campaign a political statement, which may indeed be true, because secret societies almost never remain simply workers of souls, and more often than not emerge in positions of power. The merging of secret society and secret service is for this reason a very strong one.

The brief and standard history of the Rosicrucian Brotherhood goes something like this: In or around 1615 there appeared three published manifestoes entitled "Echoes of the Fraternity of the Most Praiseworthy Order of the Rosicrucians," "Confessions of the Enigmatic Brotherhood of the Most Honourable Rose-Cross," and "The Chemical Wedding of Christian Rosenkreuz." By 1710 Samual

Richter had organized the first fraternity of the Golden Rosicrucians, and by the 19th and 20th centuries Rosicrucians were spreading far and wide.

Some believe that the alchemist Robert Fludd originated the order from a statement he made in *Tractatus apologeticus integritatem societatis Rosae Crucis defendens*: "Elijah hears the voice of God as the Rosicrucians only see the treasure at break of day.... All the mysteries of nature are open to them." The legend, however, tells us that the order was initially formed by Christian Rosenkreuz.

The symbol of the order is a seven-petal rose and a cross (usually black). The seven petals of the rose (reminding one of the number of James Bond, both as 007 and as 7777) represented something else James Bond did: secrecy. The cross symbolized the sorrows and difficulties of life. All in all one could say that James Bond was himself a symbol of this. He is the twin, the alter-ego, who deals in the secrets and sorrows of the world. There is little surprise that Rosicrucian influences seeped into the Bond novels when one understands the Rosicrucian influences upon Ian Fleming from the very earliest of times. However, Bond is also something of an individual, not a team player, and this comes across again and again in the novels.

The real secret for both Jung and Fleming would be found in the unconscious realm, and in the *Rosicrucian Chemical Wedding* both would find the sometimes-shocking imagery of the magnum opus or great work. In the book, our hero, Christian Rosenkreuz, is given information by an angel, and sets off on a quest. He undergoes a series of dangerous tests, suffers an "apocalypse," and is reborn. This mirrors the Bond novels, as both the tests and the death-rebirth are found in almost all of them, including the "chemical wedding," or the union of opposites, the sexual fusion that births the new light.

Shari'ah

The opposite of Haqiqah in Sufi tradition. Where haqiqah is the inner reality of the self, shari'ah is the outer reality.

Superconsciousness

A concept that assumes we can be more than just conscious of ourselves, but also conscious of our greater connection to the universe via being aware (conscious)—of our unconscious selves. The enlightenment process—the blinding flash of insight—is often linked to superconsciousness because individuals claim to have intense feelings of oneness with all things and incredible knowledge at a single moment in time. Unless understood properly and approached in perfect, all-encompassing balance, this often-sporadic element of the human mind can cause neurotic tendencies and psychosis—as the individual no longer feels part of society, feels god-like, has depressive mood swings, and focuses entirely on reentering the insight again.

The Unconscious

We have very little knowledge of the unconscious, because we are not conscious of it! Doorways into the world of the unconscious, as pointed out by Carl Jung and others, are dreams and lucid dreaming (being conscious of the dream).

What is held within the unconscious state are those things we as individuals have picked up all throughout our lives, and those things inherent within the mind of man, garnered over millions of years of evolution and in connection with the greater universe. This element of our unconscious world is omnipresent and identical to others'— we therefore recognize these inner archetypes when expressed outwardly by the artist, musician, writer, or speaker. Artists and others express this mystical impression because somehow (whether through drugs or a special mental connection into the world of the unconscious) they have tapped into the "source." This is often how Shamans, medicine men, priests, and prophets have sometimes appeared to "know" so much about our selves and our world.

APPENDIX B

SNAKES AND SERPENTS

Ian Fleming utilized the ancient and powerful symbol of the snake and serpent in his novels. He had them plastered on the walls at Goldeneye, as testified by Noel Coward. Fleming understood the world of the occult and alchemy, and his use of the serpent is derived from ancient sources. To better understand the role of the serpent I have included this appendix for those who have not read my other books on the subject, namely *Secrets of the Serpent, Gnosis: The Secret of Solomon's Temple Revealed,* and *The Serpent Grail*.

It is seen in the sky and on the ground, hidden in language, and glaring at us from the pages of our most profound books—the snake. In this appendix I want to journey around the world of symbols. By understanding what many of these symbols mean and just how universal they are we will be guided into this lost world of our past. We will begin with a symbol of life itself from the world's greatest ancient civilization.

Ankh

The Ankh is the Crux Ansata, a simple T-cross, surmounted by an oval called the RU, which is, simply put, the gateway to enlightenment.

This enigmatic symbol of Egypt represents eternal life, and was often found in the names of Pharaohs such as Tut-*ankh*-amun. The symbol is often depicted being held by a god in offering to a Pharaoh, giving him life, or held by a Pharaoh in offering to his people, giving them life—this basically set aside the immortals from the mortals, for anyone wearing or carrying the ankh had gained or hoped to gain immortality. Also, the pharaoh was God on earth, and so he held his own symbol of the sun and the serpent to his people—he was the sun, giving us life, just as it does in nature.

It is the loop (the RU or gateway) of the Ankh that is held by the immortals to the nostrils (as in the biblical God breathing life into the nostrils of Adam). If indeed these "immortals" are the sun, moon, and stars, then this RU device is indeed a gateway to the stars—or basically a gateway to what we were believed to return or become following death. The Ankh outlived Egyptian domination and was widely used by the Christians as their first cross, and this symbol holds a clue to the secret of the serpent.

Thoth was said to have symbolized the four elements with a simple cross, which originated from the oldest Phoenician alphabet as the curling serpent. Indeed, Philo adds that the Phoenician alphabet "are those formed by means of serpents...and adored them as the supreme gods, the rulers of the universe," thus bringing to mind the god Thoth, who again is related to the worship of serpents, and who created the alphabet. The "rulers of the universe" are indeed the planets and stars.

The T or Tau cross has been a symbol of eternal life in many cultures, and gives its name to the bull in the astrological sign of Taurus—note here the two elements of the Tau and the RU being brought together. In fact, the Druids (or "adders," after the snake) venerated the tree and the snake by scrawling the Tau cross into tree bark. In the Middle Ages, the Tau cross was used in amulets to protect the wearer against disease.

Among the modern Freemasons the Tau has many meanings. Some say that it stands for Templus Hierosolyma, or the Temple of Jerusalem; others that it signifies hidden treasure or means *Clavis ad Thesaurum*, "A key to treasure," or *Theca ubi res pretiosa*, "a place where the precious thing is concealed." It is especially important in Royal Arch Masonry, where it becomes the "Companion's Jewel," with a serpent as a circle above the cross bar—forming the Ankh with the Hebrew word for *serpent* engraved on the upright, and also including the Triple Tau—a symbol for hidden treasure.

It was also the symbol for St. Anthony—later to become the symbol for the Knights Templar of St. Anthony of Leith in Scotland. St. Anthony lived in the fourth century AD and is credited with establishing Monasticism in Egypt. The story goes that he sold all his possessions after hearing from the Lord and marched off into the wilderness to become a hermit. In his travels he learned much from various sages in Egypt and grew for himself a large following. He was sorely tempted by the devil in the form of "creeping things" and serpents (chaos). In one episode he follows a trail of gold to a temple, which is infested with serpents, and takes up residence, needing little food for sustenance other than bread and water. He is said to have lived 105 years, and due to this longevity he is credited with protective powers. The Order of the Hospitalers of St. Anthony, who would later take much of the Templar wealth, brought many of Anthony's relics to France in the 11th century, although they were said to have been secretly deposited somewhere in Egypt just after his death, and then later to have found their way to Alexandria.

The Tau or Taut symbolizes the creating four elements of the universe. Next, the symbol of the sun/serpent was added: a simple circle or the oval RU. This loop above the T cross created the ankh, the symbol of eternity. The snake in a circle eating its own tale is symbolic of the sun and immortality.

The symbol of the moon was added to this, turning it into the sign for Hermes/Mercury, and showing the caduceus/serpent origin. No wonder that this, the most perfect and simple of symbolical devices, became the symbol of the early Christians; no wonder that, even though there were no other cross-beam crucifixions, Christ was nevertheless symbolically crucified on a symbol of eternal life, a symbol of the serpent.

This symbol became the mark or sign that would set the believer aside for saving. In Ezekiel this is the mark that God will know, the mark on the forehead. The Ezekiel passage (9:4) should read, "Set a Tau upon their foreheads," or, "Mark with the letter Tau the foreheads." The early Christians baptized with the phrase *crucis thaumate notare*. They baptized with the symbol of the sun-snake. And St. Paul himself in Galatians 6:17 states, "Let no one cause me trouble, for I bear on my body the marks of Jesus."

Is this the original mark of Cain, whom we have found to be of the serpent tribe?

This sign or mark is widespread: In Job 31:35 we read in our modern bibles, "I sign now my defence—let the Almighty answer me," which should properly read, "Behold, here is my Tau, let the Almighty answer me." He then goes on and says, "Surely I would take it upon my shoulder, and bind it as a crown to me."

This remarkable idea of wearing the Tau cross on the shoulder as a sign would later become part and parcel of the crusader Templars' markings. Also, the Merovingians (said by some to be descended from Jesus and a sea serpent or fish god—the Quinotaur or Quino-Tau-rus), were supposedly born with a red cross between their shoulder blades. The Tau cross is also strangely used by those practicing sacred geometry as a marker for buried treasure, whether physical or spiritual.

Sistrum

An Egyptian musical instrument closely associated with female gods—especially Hathor, the serpent/cow goddess, and Isis, the consort of Osiris. In form it is similar to the Ankh, with a loop at the top—also representing the egg—and three serpents striking through the loop with small square pieces of metal that rattle. It's possible that these three serpents represent the pingala, ida, and sushumna nerve channels, which are said to converge and fuse together within the center of the brain (the thalamus)—which in the individual was also thought to represent the cosmic egg.

During the ascent of these serpent energies up the spine to the center of the head, the individual, while going through this supposed enlightenment process, will hear sounds similar to the sounds the sistrum makes: rattling sounds similar to tambourine bells, and sounds like a bell-tree being stroked. One will also hear sounds similar to a rattlesnake, and also whistles and flute-like instruments. Underlying these sounds is a low and strong rumbling sound that fades in at first and gets louder and louder as the process proceeds, culminating in an explosion of bright, white light in the center of the head. The sistrum then may have been a symbol of this experience.

The sistrum was used in pictures and carvings to show the various gods and pharaohs subduing the power of a particular god—and mostly because the god holding the sistrum had the power and energy to do so through having had the enlightenment experience—also representing the externalized solar power.

Birds

The association between birds or wings and the serpent seems to go back in time many thousands of years, and across the world. To quote John Bathurst Deane in *The Worship of the Serpent Traced Throughout the World*:

> The hierogram of the circle, wings, and serpent is one of the most curious emblems of Ophiolatreia, and is recognized, with some modifications, in almost every country where serpent worship prevailed.... It may be alleged that all these cannot be resolved into the single-winged serpent once coiled. Under their present form, certainly not; but it is possible that these may be corruptions of the original emblem, which was only preserved accurately in the neighbourhood of the country where the cause of serpent-worship existed; namely, in Persia, which bordered upon Babylonia and Media, the rival loci of the Garden of Eden.

Deane relates these many thousands of images of the "winged serpent" to the Seraphim of the Bible, the "flying serpents."

These could also be the origins for flying dragons, and why Quetzalcoatl was the "feathered" or "plumed serpent." The use (given by Deane) for this symbolism is for proof of deity and consecration of a given temple. If this is the case, then it was certainly believed that the ancient serpent had consecrated temples across the world. And if the serpent was a true symbol of the sun (external) and the inner light (internal), then it was a perfect fusing of our ancestors belief in one location at one time.

Dove

The dove is an important icon seen in the New Testament as a symbol of the Holy Spirit, or feminine aspect of God. It came down upon Jesus as he was baptized, giving him that famous "born again" element. It also descended upon the disciples. But why was the dove chosen?

Eurynome, probably the most important goddess of the Pelasgian myths (a people who arrived in Greece from Palestine more than 5,500 years ago), was the creator, the Mother Goddess—the ruler of all things. She was born from chaos; she separated the water from the sky and then danced across the water in order to create. While dancing she created wind or breath, and, taking hold of it between her hands, she rubbed and rubbed until she had created a snake. The snake was called Ophion, and he was filled with desire for the dancing goddess. Wrapping himself around her seven times he impregnated the her, who had now taken the form of a dove, and created an egg.

From the egg came forth all animals and plants, and Eurynome ascended to Mount Olympus to watch as her children developed. The snake Ophion bragged about his creation, so Eurynome kicked out his teeth, from which came all the people, including the first man, Pelasgus (similar to Adam), and from where the tribe derived its name. Ophion was then kicked out of heaven. The creation of the world and all that is in it was therefore again due to the snake and a goddess. But how does this goddess relate to the bird?

To the Sumerians, one of the most ancient of civilizations, she was simply known as Iahu, the "exalted Dove." This Eurynome cult had spread across the Mediterranean and became a base for many other myths and religions, including the Hebrew god Yahweh, taking on elements of the name *Lahu*. She was an original Mother Goddess, the feminine aspect, and was seen as a dove—and united with the serpent seed, she gave birth to creation.

Celtic Knotwork and Other Symbols

Due to the prevalence of the serpent in the Celtic world and surrounding cultures, it is my understanding that Celtic knotwork is derived from the images of the snake and the movements of the planets.

We can see this in the spirals and other serpent shapes seen upon many of the world's ancient monuments. In Scandinavian literature and stone art we can also see how the serpent appears, looking remarkably similar to Celtic knotwork. In Roman and Greek wall paintings there are running spirals thought to be symbolic of the protective snake.

A Neolithic vessel, now in the museum of Henan in China, shows a distinct correlation between the idea of the snake and the knotwork. The idea of the knotwork coming from the snake was probably stifled by Christian influence.

Other symbols related to the snake include the ivy leaf, a symbol of Bacchus/Dionysius and of immortality. The leaf shape is similar to the snake's head, and it entwines around pillars and trees, as the snake is shown to do in images across the world. Related to this ivy leaf image is the shape of the heart, which we can see in two Japanese clay statuettes from the Jomon period that have these snake-heart heads. Many images of the Buddha also incorporate this ivy/heart shape head—a softening and hiding of the earlier images of Naga deities who had snake heads. These ivy and heart shapes were thought to protect the person wearing them or the building adorned with them, and they are therefore no different from the concept of the protecting or guarding snake in folklore and legend. They are symbolic of the original snake—and remaineed so until Christianity demonized them.

Spirals and Other Rock Art

Spirals and carvings of snake energy are seen all over the world, as is the cult of the serpent, and it is always found to be in association with the serpent worship. According to J.C. Cooper in *An Illustrated Encyclopedia of Traditional Symbols*, the spiral "typifies the androgyne and is connected with the caduceus symbolism," which is of course the symbol of serpent healing.

Remembering that the ouroboros, the circular image of the snake eating its own tail, is an image of immortality, we should also remember the antiquity of the device. Alongside spirals are often seen circles such as the ouroboros, called "cup and ring marks." There are also zigzags, thought by many to be the fiery aspect of the serpent, and waves, showing the fluidity of the serpent—something also related to the symbolism of water. It is no surprise that such images of the snake, in all its relative forms, should be seen on the most ancient of rock art. In the cup and ring marks there are many images of what appears to be a serpent entering the cup and rings. Some have attributed this to a serpent entering a hole; others that it is eating an egg. What it definitely shows is a serpent heading toward a cup! If, of course, the snake is also the symbol of the macro sun, then these spirals and serpentine patterns may also reveal the pathways of the sun at various times of the year, and the greater years—such as those of the precession of the earth.

Spirals have been associated with astronomical alignments. This can especially be seen in the work of N.L. Thomas in *Irish Symbols of 3500 BC*, in which the spiral running right to left is seen as the winter sun, the spiral running left to right is the summer sun, and the double spiral is the spring and autumn equinox. There is little doubt, from the work carried out by Thomas, that this is true, but the fact also remains that the ancients were using symbols of the serpent in their astronomical alignments. This is matched by the fact that the serpent was seen in the sky in various constellations, and by the serpent encompassing the heavens. The two elements cannot be split apart—this was a unified theory of life, and it was created by, given life by, and kept fertile by the snake and the sun.

In Eurasia and Japan there are definite images of snakes as spirals. In earthenware from the middle Jomon period (approx. 2000 BC) of Japan these can be seen quite clearly, and are said to be there to protect the contents of the jar from harm; something important was obviously in them. Clay figures from the same period also show wound snakes. These spirals became part of family crests, and transformed in time into the yin and yang symbol of duality so popular today. These family symbols are called *kamon*, and one class of them particularly is called *janome*, which basically means "eye of the snake."

Characters for snakes in Chinese became part of the alphabet more than 3,000 years ago. Another interesting point about the snake in China is that the rainbow is said to be the snake elevated into the sky, similar to the Australian Rainbow Serpent. Indeed, the Chinese character for *rainbow* reflects this position, as it has the symbol of the snake within it.

In Peru there is pottery with spirals ending in snake heads.

In Taiwan there is a sculptured door with spirals ending in snake heads.

Swastika

The ancient symbol of the swastika is simply a stylized spiral, as can be shown from the many depictions across the world of swastikas made up of spirals and snakes. It also shows up in the spiral fashions of labyrinths and mazes. The word *labyrinth* comes directly from the ancient Minoan Snake Goddess culture of Crete, where the swastika was used as a symbol of the labyrinth and is linked etymologically with the "double-headed axe"—the Tau cross. Similar labyrinthine swastikas have been found in the ancient city of Harappa from 2000 BC. As the labyrinth is viewed as a womb of the Mother Goddess, and a symbol of the snake, there is little wonder that these two symbols became fused. Labyrinths were also seen as places of ancient serpent initiation. In ancient Egypt the labyrinth was synonymous with what was called the *amenti*—the snake-like path taken by the dead to journey from death to resurrection. It was Isis, the serpent queen of heaven, who was to guide the souls through the twists of the amenti. The path to the center leads to treasure. The snake adorning Athene in ancient Greece is shown with a swastika skirt. The same is true of Astarte and Artemis. There is Samarran pottery dating from 5000–4000 BC from Mesopotamia showing a female swastika, in which the hair swirls with Medusa-type serpents. The swastika is also shown as two serpents crossing each other.

In Norse myth, the hammer of Thor (note that *labyrinth* means double-headed axe, just like the Hammer of Thor!), Mjollnir, is closely connected with the swastika, and is found to be a prominent motif in Scandinavian art from the Bronze Age to the Iron Age. It is found on swords and Anglo-Saxon cremation urns, and on numerous Viking items. It was seen as a protector against thieves, reminiscent of the fact that serpents were known to guard treasure. As Thor's hammer was also seen as a Tau cross, it is certainly related to the secrets of the serpent. It was used by Thor to lop off the head of the sacred ox, which he used as bait to catch the Midgard Serpent, which circled the globe in the symbol of the ouroboros, eating its own tail. This was Thor offering a head as sacrifice to the serpent to try and gain immortality in the mead—the drink of the gods. Thor's aim was to gain a cauldron big enough to take the mead for the immortals, and he needed to prove his worth by fishing for the serpent.

There is evidence to prove that the myths of these Scandinavians and the Hindus are related, as the story of Thor and the Midgard Serpent closely resemble the battle between Indra and Vritra. Vritra is the great serpent that lies at the source of two rivers (the positive and negative, or male and female), as the Midgard Serpent lies beneath the sea (of the mind, and the other side of the planet where the sun goes each night). Indra slits open the belly of the serpent to release the waters and therefore fertility back to the land. Both gods, Indra and Thor, are related to the weather, both are warrior gods with a thunderbolt as a weapon, and both slay the dragon. The swastika of the serpent is a common motif in both cultures. Eventually the Christians stole both Pagan myths, and placed St. Michael and St. George in their place—both having the red serpent cross to replace the swastika.

Taautus (Taut)

Said by Eusebius to be the originator of serpent worship in Phoenicia. Sanchoniathon called Taautus a god, and says that he made the first image of Coelus and invented hieroglyphs. This links him with Hermes Trismegistus, also known as Thoth in Egypt. Taautus consecrated the species of dragons and serpents, and the Phoenicians and Egyptians followed him in this superstition.

This Taautus could very well be a memory of the group who originated the worship of the serpent after the flood or the end of the last ice age 12,000 years ago. The idea of Taautus links precisely with the stories of Thoth, who later became a great sage of Gnostic and alchemical beliefs. Thoth was deified after his death (a time that nobody knows) and given the title "the god of health" or "the god of healing." He was the prototype for Aesculapius, and was identified with Hermes and Mercury, as well as al healers, all the wise, all teachers, all saviors, all associated with the serpent for their powers, and all individuals who could map the stars and movements of time. However, it was as the healing god that Thoth was symbolized as the serpent (whereas he is normally represented with the head of an ibis and baboon).

In addition, the letter or symbol *Tau* is the first letter of *Taautus*, *Tammuz*, and *Thoth*, and is thought to be the "Mark of Cain."

►◄

So there we have many symbols and references to the sun and the snake. There are often confusing elements at play here, which often seem to mislead us and appear "hidden" because we have simply forgotten the real truth. In essence, we can reduce all of this down to three simple and distinct parts to help us on our journey.

We must remember before we do so that the very word, *snake*, is derived from both the animal and the sun—sun-ake. Now we can see clearly that the serpent was often but not solely used as a symbol of the movements of the great god in the sky—the sun. Secondly, the snake was a symbol of the internal sun—what people know of today as enlightenment. Thirdly, the real and literal snake did indeed offer up its body for our use. We created an Elixir of Life from its venom and blood, healed our skin with its skin, and brewed wonderful concoctions from its other parts.

All in all, the serpent or snake has been a powerful literal and physical element, and a useful symbolic part of our history. In fact, in all my own research I have simply not discovered a more potent and powerful symbol of multiple meanings. Ian Fleming, in using the symbols of the serpent and dragon, is revealing his understanding of this most ancient of symbolic devices.

APPENDIX C

THE NUMBER 7

In the main body of the book I often referred to the number 7 and gave some idea of its significance. A study of the use of the number is often enlightening. The following is a small collection of 7s from history and religion around the globe.

▶ In the book we have noted that Aleister Crowley wrote a book entitled *777*, and that James Bond was renumbered 7777. The number 7, and variants of it, are of the most profound importance to the world of the occult, and indeed religion, astrology, alchemy, Eastern traditions, and many more.

▶ Crowley and the various secret societies of his day, as well as Ian Fleming, used biblical and other sources for their work. In the Old Testament, Lamech lives for 777 years. From Genesis 4:19–24 (using etymological and numerological interpretations) we can paraphrase: *God's servant took two wives, light and darkness. The light brought forth the shepherd, who was the father of tent-dwellers, and herdsmen, and his brother was the musician, who was the father of harpists and pipers. But the darkness brought forth the blacksmith, the forger of brass, and of iron, and his sister was pleasure.* So, Lamech joins light and darkness, the two opposing dualities of Manichean and Gnostic thought, and the results are symbolic, and have been utilized by secret societies such as the Freemasons. Lamech loses his sight and has to be led by the son of serpents, Tubal-Cain (his son), who is of paramount importance in Freemasonic and occult lore. The Freemasons have a symbol and secret password called the "two-ball-cane," which is two balls and a cane that looks like the number 7 (070 or 007) and represents Tubal-Cain. It is also an obvious phallic symbol. Lamech is the seventh generation from Cain—the character whom we saw was "marked" on his left shoulder like James Bond.

Tubal-Cain was an artificer in metal work, and is seen as one of the first alchemists. He was the result of the union brought about by Lamech, between light and darkness, and so he is the perfected man. It was Tubal-Cain who, according to Masonic tradition, forged the pillars of Tubal-Cain later copied at the temple by Tubal-Cain's descendent Hiram Abiff as Joachim (beauty) and Boaz (strength)— JB. Great codes of wisdom were inscribed upon these pillars for future generations to discover, kept safe by Noah when he discovered them after the flood. These are claimed to be the root of all occult lore. According to Masonic lore, *Tubal-Cain* means "possessor of the world."

▶ According to Indian numerology, the number 7 fits perfectly with James Bond: mystical, intuitive, likes to work alone, great self-control and determination, and torn between the world of the rational and the world of the unconscious.

▶ There are seven sacraments: the material, or practical, being unction, marriage, penance, and the holy orders, and the spiritual triad of confirmation, baptism, and the Eucharist.

▶ The four phases of the moon change every seven days, and our ancestors saw seven planets: the sun, the moon, Mercury, Mars, Venus, Jupiter, and Saturn.

▶ The bible contains septenary design, based upon the number 7—a remarkable discovery by a man named Dr. Ivan Panin more than 50 years ago, which ago still remains virtually an untold story. Panin was a Russian, living in America. He was a brilliant mathematician, fluent in Hebrew and Greek, and an agnostic. The story goes that out of literary interest he decided to read the Old Testament in its original language. He stumbled upon what he believed to be mathematical proof that God existed.

To make a start we shall take the Hebrew alphabet. This consists of 22 letters with five finals added to make up three series of nine—or 27 letters in all. Each letter in the alphabet has a number attributed to it. For example, Aleph = 1 and Samech = 60. Therefore, when a word, sentence, paragraph, or chapter is written in Hebrew, it also carries a numerical value.

This numerical value in turn has a spiritual coding, and when the passage is broken down, different spiritual values are found for each saying, word, or name. As a few examples I have chosen the more important numbers in the Bible. Number 1 represents the beginning and unity. Number 3 means completeness or fullness. Number 7 is spiritual holiness. Number 12 is the perfection of the governing body or rulers. So we can see that within the very words of the Bible there can be a more subtle meaning or insight.

This is not unusual in itself, as Latin also has numbers attributed to its letters. Even the English language has a kind of numerology. For example, when we take the numbers that are given to the English language and work out the number for the name *Jesus Christ* we find that we get the number 7. This is then translated to mean "the mystery." What is striking is the ridiculous repetition of the number 7 or its multiples in the original Hebrew script.

Panin found that in the Hebrew Old Testament there were as many as 70 occurrences of this in every passage. From passage to passage there was an amazing overarching link of septenary design, which carried on and on throughout the whole of a single book. Also, when all the books are put together as one, the same remarkable link occurs, as if they were somehow meant to be together. Every passage of every book, and every book of the Old Testament, has this design. Nothing seems to upsets its course, not even the long lists of names, which sometimes can be laborious.

▶ What about the New Testament of the Christians?

This, the second part of the Bible, was written mainly in Greek. The alphabet, correspondingly, also has numbers attributed to them. For instance, Alpha = 1 and Upsilon = 400. Therefore, maybe it too has some kind of a design? It does. It is exactly the same as the Old Testament. But don't take just my word for it; let's look at Mark as an example.

In the last 12 verses alone there are 60 features. A few are as follows: There are 175 words (or 25 × 7); 98 words (or 2 × 7 × 7); 553 letters (or 79 × 7); 133 forms (or 19 × 7). This carries on throughout the whole of the New Testament, unbroken.

▶ It may also be of note that in English we can see a strange medieval numerology. This works by writing the numbers 1 through 9 across, and the English alphabet underneath, as follows.

1	2	3	4	5	6	7	8	9
A	B	C	D	E	F	G	H	I
J	K	L	M	N	O	P	Q	R
S	T	U	V	W	X	Y	Z	

If we write "Jesus Christ" in numbers then, we have 15131 389912, which totals 43, which we then add together to get the final total: 7. Again, as in the Hebrew and Greek, the English numbers have meanings. The number 7 means "mysterious and austere."

▶ The biblical Joshua walked around Jericho (the first civilization, according to some, and home of the largest group of Shamans) seven times. It took seven stages to bring the sinful world or lower nature crumbling down.

▶ Seven heavens are to be found in the Koran, in the Bible, and in the traditions of the Shamans and Druids. These seven heavens must also relate to the levels of enlightenment associated with the Hindu chakra system, which parallel the planets.

- There are seven *steps* to Heaven in popular belief, which can be found on many ziggurats and pyramids.

- There are seven deadly sins and seven virtues. These are methods of balancing out desires with wisdom. These are the opposite sides of the same coin—desires that must be checked.

- Life has seven cycles, according to tradition, and this emerges from the cycles of enlightenment as we grow older on the path.

- There are seven sacraments, according to the Christian Church.

- The seventh son of the seventh son is, by Jewish tradition, believed to have great healing powers.

- Magic boots, which allow the wearer to walk seven leagues in one stride, hearken back to the mythical magic of the giants or men of renown. These are the Egregores or Watchers, also known as Shining Ones.

- There are seven days in a week, which match the days in creation; the creative principle of man must follow the sevenfold path.

- The Hebraic "to swear on oath" means to come under the influence of the seven, which could possibly infer the seven planets.

- There are seven Argive heroes in Greek legend.

- There are seven champions in English legend.

- There are seven seas and seven wonders of the ancient world.

- There are seven gifts of the spirits. These are obviously linked to the seven chakra system, enlightening the spirit within.

▶ The Nagas of India worship a seven-headed snake, also seen in Sumeria atop the sacred tree.

▶ There are seven Japanese gods of luck.

▶ Mary is said to have experienced seven joys/sorrows—again the balance of opposites.

▶ In Greece there were seven sages Wise Men.

▶ There are seven sciences:

  1. Grammar.

  2. Dialectics.

  3. Rhetoric.

  4. Arithmetic.

  5. Music.

  6. Geometry.

  7. Astrology.

▶ There are seven senses—according to the ancients—under the influence of the seven planets of Classical times. These are in reality the seven "planets" within us. Fire moves; earth gives the sense of feeling; water gives speech; air, taste; mist, sight; flowers, hearing; and the south wind, smell.

▶ There are seven elementary hues to the light spectrum; when blended together they form white.

▶ We also see the theme of seven at the microcosmic level: The atom has up to seven inner orbits, called electron shells, and these seven orbits, shells, or levels reflect the levels of the electromagnetic spectrum.

><

The number 7 has been and still is to this day the most important and widespread number utilized by humankind for mystical reasons. It has found itself at the heart of religion, the occult, and even the atom. It is a number that binds things together and sets the days of the week. It is the thread throughout our time and space, and there is little wonder that Ian Fleming chose it for his hero.

Notes

Introduction

1. *Kananga* is the name of an underworld deity or a special holy water used in purification rituals, developing from African (Angolan) lore into voodoo culture. This was only the name in the film, however, and *not* the book, and is believed to be taken from an individual where filming took place.

2. Eco, *Rough Guide*, 30.

3. According to the writer Donald McCormick (alias Richard Deacon), John Dee signed his memos "007," or two eyes followed by the occult number 7, meaning he offered his physical sight and his occult sight—thus making Bond an occult agent. Ian Fleming worked with Donald McCormick in the secret service during the Second World War!

Chapter 1

1. Lee, *Lord*.

2. Pearson, *Life*.

Chapter 2

1. Eco, *Rough Guide*, 36.

2. Ibid., 45.

Chapter 3

1. Pearson, *Life*.

2. Ibid., 38.

3. Ibid., 43.

4. Ibid., 47.

5. Ibid., 53.

Chapter 4

1. *www.wikisource.org*, translated by Arthur Edward Waite, 1888.

2. *www.britflicks.com*.

3. Jaffe, *Memories*.

4. Ibid.

Chapter 6

1. *www.leninimports.com/Rudolf_hess_and_the_royals.html*.

2. Pearson, *Life*, 127.

3. Ibid.

4. Ibid., 128.

5. Ibid., 165.

6. *Http://en.wikipedia.org/wiki/Thrilling_Cities*.

7. Pearson, *Life*, 167.

8. Ibid., 172.

9. Ibid., 168.

10. Ibid., 200.

11. Ibid., 226.

12. Ibid., 227.

13. Ibid., 235.

14. Ibid., 236.

15. Ibid., 259.

16. Ibid.

17. Ibid., 246.

18. Ibid., 365.

19. Mackay, *Extraordinary*, 290.

20. *www.crcsite.org/dee1.htm*.

21. *Http://clutch.open.ac.uk/schools/emerson00/pwe_research_units.html*.

Chapter 7

1. Lycett, *Ian Fleming*.

2. Within, *Trail*, 206.

3. Fleming, *Dr. No*.

4. Translated in 1997 by Scott J. Thompson. See *www.wbenjamin.org*.

5. Whitegead, "The Prisoner."

6. Ibid.

7. Pearson, *Life*, 226.

Chapter 8

1. Pearson, *Life*, 327.

Chapter 9

1. Lycett, *Ian Fleming*.

2. Ibid., 340.

3. Pearson, *Life*.

Chapter 10

1. Jung, *Psychology*.

2. Jaffe, *Memories*, 200.

3. Ibid., 192–193.

4. Hoeller, "C.G. Jung."

5. Ibid.

6. Ibid.

7. Ellman and O'Clair, *Norton Anthology*, 449.

8. "Edith Sitwell."

9. Ibid.

10. Ibid.

11. Ravin, "Sybil Leek."

12. Wooley, *Queen's*, 38.

13. Ibid., 71.

14. Ibid., 14.

15. Howard, *Occult*, 136.

Chapter 11

1. There are many arguments about the Mark of Cain. Some claim that it was black skin, and this was utilized for racist purposes, but the esoteric belief is a Shamanic mark upon the hand or shoulder.

2. Rees, *Just Six*, 55.

3. Ibid., 57.

Appendix A

1. Jaffe, *Memories*, 391.

BIBLIOGRAPHY

Ableson, J. *Jewish Mysticism*. London: G Bell and Sons Ltd., 1913.

Andrews, R., and P. Schellenberger. *The Tomb of God*. London: Little, Brown, and Co., 1996.

Ashe, Geoffrey. *The Quest for Arthur's Britain*. London: Paladin, 1971.

Baigent, Michael, and Richard Leigh. *The Temple and the Lodge*. London: Arrow, 1998.

Balfour, Mark. *The Sign of the Serpent*. London: Prism, 1990.

Barrett, David. *Sects, Cults and Alternative Religions*. London: Blandford, 1996.

Bayley, H. *The Lost Language of Symbolism*. London: Bracken Books, 1996.

Blavatsky, H.P. *Theosophical Glossary*. Whitefish, Mont.: R.A. Kessinger Publishing Ltd., 1918.

Borchant, Bruno. *Mysticism*. Centennial, Colo.: Weisner, 1994.

Bord, Colin, and Janet Bord. *Earth Rites: Fertility Practices in Pre-Industrial Britain*. London: Granada Publishing, 1982.

Bouquet, A.C. *Comparative Religion*. London: Pelican, 1942.

Bradley, Michael. *The Secret Societies Handbook*. London: Cassell, 2005.

Carr-Gomm, Sarah. *Dictionary of Symbols in Art*. London: Duncan Baird Publishers, 1995.

Clarke, Hyde, and C. Staniland Wake. *Serpent and Siva Worship*. Whitefish, Mont.: R.A. Kessinger Publishing Ltd., 1877.

Cooper, J.C. *An Illustrated Encyclopaedia of Traditional Symbols*. London: Thames and Hudson, 1978.

Davidson, H.R. Ellis. *Myths and Symbols of Pagan Europe*. Syracuse, N.Y.: Syracuse University Press, 1988.

Deacon, Richard. *John Dee: Scientist, Geographer, Astrologer and Secret Agent to Elizabeth I*. London: Frederick Muller, 1968.

Deane, John Bathurst. *The Worship of the Serpent Traced Throughout the World: Attesting the Temptation and Fall of Man by the Instrumentality of a Serpent Tempter, Second Edition*. Unknown city and publisher, 1833.

Eco, Umberto. *The Rough Guide to James Bond*. London: Haymarket Publishing, 2002.

"Edith Sitwell: A Nearly Forgotten Poetess." Paper from the Arkansas School for Mathematics and Sciences, 1997. *http://asms.k12.ar.us/classes/humanities/brtitlit/97-98/sitwell/Sitwell.htm*.

Ellman, Richard, and Robert O'Clair, eds. *The Norton Anthology of Modern Poetry*. London: W.W. Norton and Company, 1988.

Ferguson, Diana. *Tales of the Plumed Serpent*. London: Collins and Brown, 2000.

Fleming, Ian. *Casino Royale*. London: Pan Books, 1964.

———. *Diamonds Are Forever*. London: Pan Books, 1956.

———. *Dr. No*. London: Pan Books, 1958.

———. *For Your Eyes Only*. London: Pan Books, 1969.

———. *From Russia With Love*. London: Pan Books, 1957.

———. *Goldfinger*. London: Pan Books, 1959.

———. *Live and Let Die*. London: Pan Books, 1954.

———. *The Man With the Golden Gun*. London: Pan Books, 1965.

———. *Moonraker*. London: Pan Books, 1955.

———. *Octopussy*. London: Pan Books, 1966.

———. *On Her Majesty's Secret Service*. London: Pan Books, 1963.

———. *The Spy Who Loved Me*. London: Pan Books, 1962.

———. *Thunderball*. London: Pan Books, 1961.

———. *You Only Live Twice*. London: Pan Books, 1964.

Fontana, David. *The Secret Language of Symbols*. London: Piatkus, 1997.

Fortune, Dion. *The Mystical Qabalah*. New York: Weiser Books, 2000.

Gardiner, Philip. *Gnosis: The Secret of Solomon's Temple Revealed*. Franklin Lakes, N.J.: New Page Books, 2006.

———. *Secrets of the Serpent*. Los Angeles: Reality Press, 2006.

Harrington, E. *The Meaning of English Place Names*. Belfast, Ireland: The Black Staff Press, 1995.

Hoeller, Stephan A. "C.G. Jung and the Alchemical Renewal." *www.gnosis.org/jung_alchemy.htm* (accessed February 2008).

Howard, M. *The Occult Conspiracy*. Rochester, N.Y.: Destiny Books, 1989.

Jaffe, Aniela, ed. *Memories, Dreams, Reflections of C.G. Jung*. New York: Vintage, 1963.

Jennings, Hargrave. *Ophiolatreia*. Whitefish, Mont.: Kessinger Publishing Ltd., 1996.

Jones, Alison. *Dictionary of World Folklore*. New York: Larousse, 1995.

Jung, Carl. *My Life*. In *Collected Works*, edited by Herbert Read, Michael Fordham, and Gerard Adler, translated by R.F.C. Hull. New York: Pantheon, 1953.

———. *Psychology and Literature*. Princeton, N.J.: Princeton University Press, 1966.

Kauffeld, Carl. *Snakes: The Keeper and the Kept*. London: Doubleday and Co., 1969.

Lapatin, Kenneth. *Mysteries of the Snake Goddess*. Boston: Houghton Mifflin, 2002.

Lee, Christopher. *Lord of Misrule: The Autobiography of Christopher Lee*. London: Orion, 2004.

Levi, Eliphas. *Transcendental Magic*. London: Tiger Books, 1995.

Lycett, Andrew. *Ian Fleming*. London: Phoenix, 1995.

Mackay, Charles. *Extraordinary Popular Delusions and the Madness of Crowds*. London: Wordsworth, 1995.

Mann, A.T. *Sacred Architecture*. London: Element, 1993.

Oliver, George. *Signs and Symbols*. New York: Macoy Publishing, 1906.

Pearson, John. *The Life of Ian Fleming*. London: Aurum, 2003.

Pennick, N. *Sacred Geometry*. Chievely, UK: Capall Bann, 1994.

Pike, Albert. *The Morals and Dogma of Scottish Rite Freemasonry*. London: L.H. Jenkins, 1928.

Rabten, Geshe. *Echoes of Voidness*. London: Wisdom Publications, 1983.

Radin, Dean. *The Conscious Universe*. London: HarperCollins, 1997.

Ravin, C. "Sybil Leek: 20th Century Witch-Astrologer." *www.lovestarz.com/leek.html* (accessed February 2008).

Read, Anthony. *The Devil's Disciples: The Lives and Times of Hitler's Inner Circle*. London: Pimlico, 2003.

Rees, Martin. *Just Six Numbers*. London: Phoenix, 2000.

Rinpoche, Lati, Denma Locho Rinpoche, Leah Zahler, and Jeffrey Hopkins. *Meditative States in Tibetan Buddhism*. London: Wisdom Publications, 1983.

Roberts, J.M. *The Mythology of the Secret Societies*. London: Granada, 1972.

Russell, Peter. *The Brain Book*. London: Routledge, 1980.

S, Acharya. *The Christ Conspiracy: The Greatest Story Ever Sold*. Stelle, Ill.: AVP, 2003.

Scott, Ernest. *The People of the Secret*. London: The Octagon Press, 1983.

Sharper Knowlson, T. *The Origins of Popular Superstitions and Customs*. London: Senate, 1994.

Simpson, Paul, ed. *The Rough Guide to James Bond*. London: Haymarket, 2002.

Snyder, Louis L. *Encyclopaedia of the Third Reich*. London: Wordsworth, 1998.

Stone, Nathan. *Names of God*. Chicago: Moody, 1944.

Taylor, Richard. *How to Read a Church*. London: Random House, 2003.

Thomson, Ahmad. *Dajjal the Anti-Christ*. London: Ta-Ha Publishers Ltd., 1993.

Thomson, Oliver. *Easily Led: A history of Propaganda*. Gloucestershire, UK: Sutton Publishing, 1999.

Toland, John. *Hitler*. London: Wordsworth, 1997.

Wake, C. Staniland. *The Origin of Serpent Worship*. Whitefish, Mont.: R.A. Kessinger Publishing Ltd, 1877.

Walker, B. *Gnosticism*. Wellingborough, UK: Aquarian Press, 1983.

Weber, Renee. *Dialogues with Scientists and Sages: Search for Unity in Science and Mysticism*. London: Arkana, 1990.

Weisse, John. *The Obelisk and Freemasonry*. Whitefish, Mont.: R.A. Kessinger Publishing Ltd., 1996.

Whitegead, John W. "The Prisoner of the Mind." March 29, 2006. *www.prisonplanet.com/articles/march2006/290306prisoner.htm* (accessed February 2008).

Within, Enquire. *Trail of the Serpent*. Publisher, author (supposedly "Enquire Within"), and date kept a secret.

Woolley, Benjamin. *The Queens's Conjuror*. London: HarperCollins, 2001.

Yates, Frances Amelia. *Majesty and Magic in Shakespeare's Last Plays*. Boulder, Colo.: Shambhala, 1978.

Index

A

Accidie, 149

Adler, Alfred, 55-58

Age of Reason, 127

"Agnosticism," 126

Agrippa, Cornelius, 64, 107

Albigenses, 119

Alchemy, 10, 11-13, 14, 37, 39-40, 48, 65, 69-72, 74-75, 77, 85-86, 87, 93, 105, 110, 116, 127, 129, 145, 155, 159, 172, 187

Amis, Kingsley, 25

analytical psychiatry, 74

Animal Farm, 151

Anu, 79

Apologia Alchymiae, 172

Archidoxes of Magic, 64

Areopolis, 36

Ark of the Covenant, the, 67, 192

Ark, The Shroud, and Mary, The, 8

Armitage, Selby, 61

Arthur, King, 67-69, 81, 85, 150-151, 188

Asherah poles, 79-80

Asherim, 80

astrology, 38, 115-116, 164

B

Bacon, Francis, 107

Bagnold, Enid, 105-106

balance, 66, 79, 97-98, 104, 132, 144

Baphomet, 93, 95

Basilisk, Sable, 47

Benjamin, Walter, 125-126

Bennett, Allan, 174-175

Besant, Annie, 111

Bey, Darko Kerim, 190

Big, Mr., 15-16, 33, 35, 37-38, 149, 183-184, 189

birth order, 57

black magic, 178-179

Black Mass, 152

black propaganda, 114-115

Blanshard, Clare, 145

Blavatsky, Helena, 88

Bleuville, 46

Blofeld, Ernst Stavro, 44, 46, 48-49, 124, 187-188

Bloom, Howard, 180

Bloomsbury
Black Mass, 106-107, 152
Set, 106, 107, 111, 152

Blunt,
Anthony, 106
Irma, 124

Boaz, 122, 192

Bond, Tracey, 187, 188

Book of the Law, The, 175

Bord, Gustav, 110

Bottome, Phyllis, 21, 57-58

Braid, James, 128

Brand, Gala, 38-39

Bricaud, J., 152

British Secret Service and 17F, 89-90

Broccoli, Albert R. "Cubby," 25

Brood of the Witch Queen, 171-172

Brosnan, Pierce, 30, 38, 92

Brothers of St. John of Jerusalem, 119

Bryce, Ivar, 92-93

Buchan, John, 150, 180

Buddhism, 146-147

Burgess, Gary, 106

C

Cainites, 154, 193

Calvin, John, 122-123

Cambridge
Apostles, 106
Spy Ring, 106

Campbell, Martin, 30

Cascariolo, Vincenzo, 124

Case, Tiffany, 39, 190

Casino Royale, 15-16, 24, 30-33, 100-104, 128, 135, 145-146, 149, 168-169, 190, 193

Cathars, 119, 154

Catholic Church, 8-9, 66, 78, 81

cell structure, 98-99

Chandler, Raymond, 25

chemistry, 65, 127

Chiffre, Le, 16, 30-33, 102-103, 146, 149

Chitty Chitty Bang Bang, 10, 15, 25, 160, 169

Churchill, Winston, 54, 89, 90-91, 114, 161, 175

CIA, 23

Cisterians, 81

Cold War, the, 129

collective unconscious, the, 100, 158

Commercial Intelligence, 170

Connery, Sean, 25, 30, 192

Connolly, Cyril, 25

consciousness, 37, 77, 163

Councell, Dr. R. Watson, 171

Coward, Noel, 25, 98, 139-140

Craig, Daniel, 30

Crowley, Aleister, 14, 32-34, 48, 87-88, 90-92, 103, 106, 113, 134, 154-155, 161, 163-165, 168-169, 171, 173-177, 178-179

Crusades, the, 81

Golden Dawn, Order of the, 112, 161, 171, 173-176, 186

golden proportion, the, 95

Goldeneye, 15, 96, 128, 143

Goldeneye, 30, 92-93

Goldfinger, 29, 42-43, 186

Goldfinger, Auric, 15, 42, 186-187

Goodnight, Mary, 50

gravity, 195-196

Great Beast, 91

Green Eyes of Bast, 172

Grey Face, 172

Guide to Magic, Witchcraft and the Paranormal, The, 173

Guinevere, 67-69, 81, 188

H

Hamilton, Duke of, 89, 90

Hardy, Thomas, 164

Heindel, Max, 112

Henry VIII, King, 107

heretics, 8

Hermes, 154

Hermetic philosophy, 64

Hess, Rudolf, 87-92, 114, 115

Hildebrand Rarity, The, 43, 85

Himmler, 115

Hitler, Adolf, 87-90, 115

Hohenheim, Theophrastus Philippus Aureolus Bombastas von, 63

Holmes, Sherlock, 151, 180

Holy Grail, the, 10, 35, 67, 81, 132, 150

Hoover, J, Edgar, 22

horizon list, 99

Horus, 36, 95, 175

Howard, Edward, 126

Michael, 179

hundredth monkey principle, 101

Hutton, James, 126

Huxley, T.H., 126

Hyaster, 84

Hylaster, 159

hypnagogic state, 134

hypnotism, 128

I

Ian Fleming, 145, 149

Illuminati, 111

Inner Manu, 36

Ishtar, 80

Isis, 80

J

Joachim, 122, 192

John, Augustus, 55

Jung, Carl, 13-14, 45, 56, 61-62, 65-70, 72-77, 78, 81-86, 98, 100-101, 104, 144, 146-147, 155, 157-161

Just Six Numbers, 194

K

Kafka, 58

Kananga, 10, 16, 184

Kell, Vernon, 177

Kelly, Edward and Rose Edith, 175

Kennedy, John F., 40

Kennedys, the, 25

Keyes, Roger, 164

Klebb, Rosa, 41

Knight, Maxwell, 177-180

Knights of Malta, 47

Temple of
    Jerusalem, 133
    Solomon, 79, 192
30 AU, 23-24
39 Steps, 180
Thrilling Cities, 58, 147
"Thrilling Cities," 96-97
Thule Society, 88
Thunderball, 43-44, 50, 187, 192
Times, 21, 24, 27, 99
Todoroki, Taro, 49, 192
Traveller's Tree, The, 35, 36
Tree of Life and Knowledge, 80
Trithemious, 167
twin pillars, 122

U

umbrella motif, 133
unconscious realm, 42
Unholy Alliance, 179
Ustinov, Peter, 141

V

Valentine, Basil, 172
Vicenzo, Teresa de, 46-47
Victoria, Queen, 53, 168
Vincenzo,
    Guido di, 124
    Teresa di, 124
Vitali, Dominetta, 44
Von Hofmannsthal, 58
Voodoo, 33, 36-37, 97, 184

W

Waite, A.E., 113
Walsingham, Francis, 168
Ward, Arthur Henry, 169, 173
water deities, 45-46
Watkins, Geoffrey, 113-114, 160-161
Waugh, Evelyn, 148
Weishaupt, Adam, 111
Wells, H.G., 164
Westcott, Dr. Wynn, 111
Wheatley, Dennis, 14, 115, 179
White Cliffs, 140
White Stains, 174
Whitegead, John, 133
Wilhelm, Richard, 77
Williams-Ellis, Clough, 134
Witchcraft, 163-165
Wohl, Louis de, 115-116
Wohl-Musciny, Ludwig Von, 115-116
(Wonderful) Wizard of Oz, The, 10

Y

Yahweh, 79, 80
Yates, Francis, 167
Yeats, W.B., 113, 161, 171, 174
yin and yang, 77
You Only Live Twice, 47-49, 50, 192

Z

"Zayat Kiss," 171
zodiac, 64
Zweig, 58

About the Author

Philip Gardiner is the best-selling author of several books, including *Gnosis: The Secret of Solomon's Temple Revealed; The Ark, The Shroud, and Mary; Secret Societies; Secrets of the Serpent;* and *Gateways to the Otherworld.* He has made numerous documentary films, has appeared on television and radio hundreds of times, and speaks across the world, from Australia to the United States. His Website is *www.gardinersworld.com.*